DESCENT

OF A

BROKEN
MAN

ASHON RUFFINS

Copyright © 2022 by Ashon Ruffins and Dreadful Times Press, LLC
Edited by: Chelsea Terry (Stand Corrected Editing)
         Nichole Heydenburg (Poisoned Ink Press)
         Roxana Coumans (Roth Notions)
Cover Design by: Fay Lane Graphic Design
Book Design by: Eliott Designs

ISBN 979-8-9855902-0-3

First printing 2022

For Kenyatta, Taylor, and Ashon.
You are my anchors in the storm.

-A.R.

DESCENT

OF A

BROKEN

MAN

CHAPTER
ONE

"I'm not going anywhere without you right next to me."
—Damon

1994

"Oh my god, that was terrible!" Cynthia said as she gripped Damon's hand and crossed an intersection on Canal St. "I can't believe I let you talk me into watching that. They actually made two of those?"

"Man, that movie was funny as hell!" he said chuckling; his smile widened to its limits.

Damon had one of those million-dollar smiles that displayed two perfect rows of pearly white teeth. Cynthia blushed at the sight of him. Her cheeks flushed as she smiled back at him and she found herself resisting the urge to agree with him to watch him smile a little longer. The sight of his smile caused her heart to flutter and she giggled softly.

"Damon, it's supposed to be a scary movie. Although, why anybody would choose to make a damn leprechaun scary is beyond me," Cynthia said, shaking her head, as she peeked down at her Mickey Mouse wristwatch. A wave of disappointment overwhelmed her when she realized she had wasted more than an hour watching the flick. "Ugh, all these people. Why don't they stay home?"

Cynthia and Damon weaved through the thick crowd of colorful costumed tourists dressed in a variety of provocative outfits. The crowd of intoxicated people clogged the entire sidewalk in their journey for inadvertent alcohol poisoning and holiday debauchery.

The young couple hustled across the lively street after enjoying a night to themselves after final exams of their senior year of high school.

Cynthia glanced over her shoulder as she trailed Damon and noticed the brilliant lights that circled the sign of the Joy Theater. The black sky behind the venue acted as the perfect backdrop that created a striking contrast. The photographic scene forced fanciful thoughts of the skyline of Times Square, a sight Cynthia had often dreamed of witnessing if provided the chance. The movie theater's sign stretched for about twenty feet, and the large, incandescent light bulbs that outlined the name shimmered in the night.

Cynthia wondered how long it would be before it fell apart like the rest of New Orleans. She supposed that the New York signs were taller and brighter.

Cynthia and Damon continued their way down the walkway, their fingers instinctively intertwined to ensure they didn't get separated in the crowd. Damon stopped and turned every few yards, enticed by the touch of Cynthia's soft skin, compelled to demonstrate his passion for her with a kiss. Through all the clamor, both managed to hear each other through the large overflow of festival goers and laughed at the tourists taking advantage of the 24-hour drinking culture of the city. Damon's eyes lit up as he stopped by one of the only tourist voodoo shops along Canal St.

"Check this out, baby!" Damon said as he grabbed a book from the circular rack sitting out front. "The history of New Orleans and its most famous haunted houses, monsters and murderers. Oh, man. I have to get this. Look, it even talks about the New Orleans Axe murderer, Madam LaLaurie, and all the haunted places in the Quarter."

"Damon, what is it with you and the fascination with horror? It's a little weird, baby."

"Look at these people, babe. They come here for all types of reasons. Yeah, most just want to get fucked up, but a lot of them visit for the history, music and the culture. Along with it all, the history is laden with lore of the macabre and tales of the supernatural. It's kinda cool to think about the other things the city is known for besides the crime, the corruption and Bourbon St.," he responded.

"This doesn't sound like the man I've been with a couple of

years. My honey couldn't wait to leave this city. Sounds to me like you are having second thoughts on going away for school?"

"No. Not at all. You know how it is, Cyn. The city becomes a part of you, but we need to get out of here. Enjoy other places and see other things."

However extraordinary the city, Cynthia and Damon were not interested in any of it in the long term. The thought of escaping New Orleans and the violence of their hometown after graduation excited their youthful minds. Ever mindful, Cynthia watched her surroundings and stayed aware of some of the dangers in the area, but the pair managed to enjoy their brisk walk among the tourists before they made it to a much thinner crowd and a much rougher neighborhood.

"Jesus, it's too early in the year to be this hot," Cynthia complained, as she fanned herself with her hand.

"No shit. I wish we didn't have to wait until the fall semester to get to Colorado. You know how hot it gets down here in the summer, and there'll be a lot of bodies because of it," Damon replied.

"The dope man will be out this summer and I don't wanna be anywhere near him. Can we just spend the summer inside under each other, out of the heat, and away from the drama?" he asked with a bit of a sly look on his face.

"I can't believe what I'm hearing. You spent most of our senior year playing pranks and fucking with people, and now you want to sit inside and behave yourself?" she asked with a smirk.

"I have to see those snow-topped mountains. Get away from the streets of New Orleans and all the damn killing," he reasoned. His grip of her hand tightened while he spoke. "We're gonna go down Basin St. because it's faster."

"No! Let's walk up a block," Cynthia insisted. "I don't wanna walk past the project. It's too dark and too late for that shit."

"I'm not going anywhere without you right next to me. Look, we'll walk on the other side of the street," said Damon with his smile. "I gotta look after my hot girl!"

As the young couple's pace quickened, two large Rottweilers snarled. Drool fell from the dogs' mouths at the sight of them, as they walked past the housing development.

"Just keep walking, baby. Don't make eye contact. They'll leave us alone," Damon insisted.

The dogs sprinted toward them, baring their teeth and leaving a trail of saliva behind them.

"Oh shit, bae! Run!" Damon yelled.

Cynthia snatched her hand away from Damon and took off toward the police station ahead. Damon beamed and raced behind Cynthia as the dogs caught up to him. The sound of the chattering teeth nipping at his heels pushed his legs faster. The vicious hounds chased and snarled after them as they sped up the block and past the First Precinct Police Station. The sound of their laughter echoed in the night's air the entire way.

Cynthia and Damon managed to lose the dogs, after they turned and entered the side gates of Louis Armstrong Park, a shortcut to their Treme neighborhood where Damon lived.

The struggle to catch their breaths while guffawing at their experience brought some lively energy to the park's dreary atmosphere.

"My God, you are so slow!" Cynthia yelled out, weak from laughter.

"Shut up!" Damon replied. "I was gonna catch you. Not really though. I tried. Your ass is too fast. I could've run behind that ass all night though."

"Boy, you play too much!" Cynthia replied, as she playfully slapped Damon softly on his cheek.

Both still hunched over with their hands on their knees as they tried to catch their breath.

"Hey, will you shut up? People are trying to sleep out here," a voice bellowed from nearby.

"Oh, shit." Damon snickered. "Now we are waking up the bums."

While Cynthia and Damon flirted, they stood under the large oak trees near Congo Square. Sweat dripped from their foreheads from the muggy evening, but the still trees above offered no sign of a breeze to break up the oppressively thick air.

The young couple continued their walk through Armstrong Park as they listened to the sound of soft jazz pumped from speakers from the nearby radio station.

As they passed the old Municipal Auditorium, a place of concerts and graduations, Damon gripped Cynthia's hand once more and pulled her toward him. The two embraced and shared a long passionate kiss under the towering presence of the oak trees.

Damon placed both hands on Cynthia's arms and caressed her smooth skin with his thumbs. Their love had grown since their sophomore year. Cynthia's hands lay upon both sides of his face, and the engagement ring on Cynthia's hand glimmered as it managed to capture the little light in the area.

As they stared into each other's eyes, a sudden movement from above caught Damon's attention.

He looked up into the sturdy wooden structures and noticed a shadowy figure hidden among the cluster of branches that rustled and swayed. A human-like figure moved with a purpose from tree to tree and bent the branches along the way, as if a hurricane force wind blew them about.

The sound of a stick snapping startled Cynthia. Damon held her hand firmly and proceeded to pull his fiancée through the park.

Cynthia glanced behind them as they hurried through the darkness, and she dipped her eyebrows with confusion at the sight of the branches breaking and falling to the ground.

As Damon yanked on Cynthia's arm, something fell from the tree before them. Damon and Cynthia halted and looked on with horror in their wide eyes.

"What the hell?" Damon mumbled as he stared ahead. Paralyzed by fear, he squeezed Cynthia's hand tighter.

She grimaced in pain, as the couple glared at the enormous figure that panted in the shadows. Its skin appeared blistered and thick, and its muscular arms hung low, almost to its knees, accompanied with sharp claws. The creature squatted and spread its claws upon the ground and stared as if it was hunting like some sort of jungle predator.

"Baby, let's...let's get out of here!" Cynthia stuttered; her voice drowned out by the close proximity of jazz music in the background.

The figure glowered at them with bright yellow eyes that pierced through the dimly-lit night.

"What is that?" Cynthia asked, her heart pounding in her chest.

Damon and Cynthia tried to turn and run away from the unnatural beast, but the figure pulled Damon away from Cynthia. The sound of something snapped behind her.

Damon's head wilted to the side and his lifeless eyes dropped open as blood poured from his mouth.

Cynthia briefly turned away from Damon's face in horror, but she couldn't look away from the love of her life in need, only to see what looked like a disfigured massive hand covered in blood protruding from his chest.

Her shrill scream filled the park and echoed loud enough to wake the dead. Cynthia tried to flee, but the grotesque monster reached out with its other hand with asphalt type skin and razor-sharp claws and slashed open Cynthia's throat. Crimson sprayed and poured out of the slit, and her body plummeted to the ground. The beast growled with sadistic satisfaction and let go of Damon's lifeless body. His corpse smacked into the concrete next to Cynthia's and he lay wide-eyed, staring at his murdered lover. Cynthia's mouth twitched repeatedly as she gasped her last breaths until her eyes closed for the final time.

The shadowy figure fled into the cover of night, silent in its movements, and the young couple's pool of blood became one.

CHAPTER TWO

"Well, good morning. What do we have, Sergeant?"
– Detective Maor

As dawn approached, the reflection of police lights covered the area and a patrolman of the New Orleans Police Department blocked off the area with yellow crime scene tape.

"Man, I've seen nothing like this," one of the patrolmen whispered to another in the background.

"That's some sick shit, brother," the other replied. "These thugs are getting worse. Is it not good enough to shoot each other anymore?"

As the double murder occurred inside the park, the crime scene remained a secret from the public, so no one crowded around for a closer look or to take photos, which simplified the First Responders' job to secure the scene.

"Hey, did any of you notify IU to get the detective out here?" an NOPD Sergeant asked.

"Yeah, Serge! She's already on her way," one officer replied.

"Good. She's going to love this shit," the Sergeant mumbled with sarcasm.

In the distance, an unmarked city vehicle approached and parked close to the scene. The person inside spoke into a police radio and recorded some notes before opening the car door. A short woman wearing army boots stepped out of the vehicle and made eye contact with the Sergeant on scene. She marched over to him. Her eyes scanned the area as she raised one eyebrow higher than the other.

"Well, good morning. What do we have, Sergeant?" she questioned in a stern, focused voice.

CHAPTER THREE

"I hope you still are, sir. I'm still trying."
—James

SEVERAL WEEKS EARLIER

As I pulled into the parking lot, the familiar sound of the gravel buckling under the tires triggered discomfort in the pit of my stomach. The thought of faking my mood to get through the day only caused anxiety and drained my energy before I stepped out of the car. Regardless, a facade was better than an explanation. When I talked about my struggle, it always ended with the same result— a look of pity, doubt, or even laughter. There was no way I needed that in the workplace.

My assigned parking spot faced the prominent name mounted on the front of the building.

"Robert E. Lee High School," I said, shaking my head in disgust, as I had so many times before. Another school in the South named after a racist confederate soldier. The feeling was too familiar, as I graduated from a similar school.

The irony was not lost on me. I watched clusters of darker-hue students and staff enter with pride, as they attended a school named after a person who fought to keep them enslaved. Few were outraged by it, probably because no one paid much attention.

"Doesn't matter right now. I have bills to pay. Besides, I have enough to deal with without thinking about that bullshit," I mumbled as I laid my head back on the head rest.

The sight of the student's horseplay and the engagement of the faculty made me envious. I couldn't feel normal. It didn't matter how hard I tried.

After dawdling and daydreaming, I glared at the briefcase on the passenger side seat. The feel of the smooth black leather always reminded me of my late father who gifted the briefcase to me on the day of my graduation. Although, the best part of the gift was tucked away inside.

The words *I'm proud of you, son* were inscribed on the gold plaque on the briefcase right below my name... James Corbin.

I hope you're still proud of me, sir. I'm still trying. I know you would understand how hard it is to fight through this.

The door handle was cool to the touch as I wrapped my fingers around it, trying to will myself to open the door. I took in a couple of deep breaths to settle my stomach and slow my breathing.

It didn't take much to trigger my anxiety but being late for a position I hated would do the job just fine. I imagined myself teaching at a university level, molding more responsive and invested minds in my favorite subjects: religion, history, and a bit of the supernatural to help motivate myself. Although, I would keep the latter topics for more open-minded company.

Years of study on these subjects ignited a passion to pass that knowledge on to other interested and more focused minds. I looked at it as a means to leave my impression in this world, remembered by the pupils I taught. That was not what I had accomplished so far. My teaching career had been boiled down to repeating dates and facts about the Revolutionary War to a bunch of hormonal, undisciplined sixteen-year-olds. Important, but not what I desired from life at the time. Plus, they weren't interested in learning.

I knew they were only teenagers, but how could anyone take some of the most influential events in history for granted? I thought.

Of course, the textbooks were mostly lies and half-truths, but I tried to slip in the factual accounts of whatever topic I covered, while trying not to piss off the principal.

Knock. Knock. Knock. The delicate taps on the window from the fleshy knuckles startled me and forced me to focus as I sat up and rolled down the window, cranking the handle vigorously.

"Hi, Mrs. Gibson. How are you this morning?"

"Good morning, Mr. Corbin. Judging by the smile on your face, it looks like you're having a good morning," she said; her elderly voice shook. "Mrs. Wilson has been talking an awful lot about you. I think you might want to walk the straight and narrow for a few weeks. Maybe point that smile of yours her way a couple of times a day."

"Thanks for the heads up. I'll give it a try. How do you manage to put up with her all day in the office together?"

"Mr. Corbin, I've been on this earth too long to let some old bag upset me. Besides, I'm too busy pushing paperwork to worry about her or her attitude," she said with a smirk. "Now don't sit here too long. The bell will be ringing soon."

"Yes, ma'am." I waved as she left.

As she walked off, the smile immediately fell from my face. My hands paled as I gripped the steering wheel a little tighter. The thought of staying in my car was appealing, but as soon as that thought comforted me, the repeated dings of the chiming bell pushed me to leave.

I exited my car with a heavy sigh and rushed to the nearest set of double doors that led to my classroom.

Before I could reach the second hallway past the administrative office, a well-dressed woman leaned against the tan-colored brick wall and glared at her watch.

"Late again, Mr. Corbin!" she yelled, sneering up at me through her thick bifocals.

"I-I'm sorry, Mrs. Wilson. Won't happen again," I replied. I continued to dart down the hallway toward my class.

"Bullshit," she conceded under her breath as the distance between her and I extended, but it was still loud enough for me to hear.

"God, I can't keep fucking up like this," I mumbled.

My propensity for vulgarity slipped through once again. I read somewhere that the use of curse words was a sign of intelligence. Although, I'm not sure if I used that bit of information for an excuse or if it was genuinely true. Either way, I had to stop letting it slip in the halls of the school.

A brief pause was needed outside the classroom door to gather myself and wipe the sweat from my brow. I breathed deeply to calm any anxiety and opened the door.

I can't keep doing this. I can't let this thing, this darkness, stop me from reaching my dreams. This is unprofessional.

"Get it together, James," I whispered. "You're better than this."

I pushed open the door to the classroom full of kids in every seat.

"Good morning, class. Welcome to World History," I greeted in an assertive tone. The smell of chalk sparked memories of nostalgia every time I entered the classroom.

"No, we welcome *you* to World History, Mr. C! You're the one who's late," a young man jested.

The entire class burst into laughter.

"Nevertheless, let's get started," I dismissed.

Before I started the lecture, my heart thumped, and my palms sweated with anticipation. Sharing my knowledge usually helped any depression or anxiety that had a hold on me.

"Today, class, we will discuss the Nubian Empire and their influence in history. I think you guys will find this very interesting. Nubia was an ancient region in northeastern Africa, extending approximately from the Nile River Valley eastward to the shores of the Red Sea. Nubia was traditionally divided into two regions. The southern portion, which extended north to the southern end of the second cataract of the Nile, was known as Upper Nubia. This was called Kush, under the 18th dynasty pharaohs of ancient Egypt, and was called Ethiopia by the ancient Greeks."

The students' eyes glazed over in disinterest. Even those who wanted to be interested had their attention elsewhere early on.

I sighed heavily and tapped the chalk on the counter in front of me as I watched the students fidget in their chairs. I proceeded with what usually provoked a reaction with any group of people, social classification and religion. Anything to get a response from them.

"How many of you know that the Nubians, just like the Egyptians, were darker in skin tone and also conquered Egypt at a certain point in history?" I asked with a louder voice.

"Yes! We know, Mr. Corbin. They were black. Like most of the people of Africa," one student sarcastically replied.

"Correct!" I responded. "Also, Nubia is believed to have served as a trade corridor between Egypt and tropical Africa long before 3100 BC. Egyptian artisans of the period used ivory and ebony wood from tropical Africa, which came through Nubia. We're talking major economic activity. So much so that trade missions took place between the two nations, causing them to become very wealthy. This even caused Nubia to expand into sub nations that shared technology, pottery techniques, and even social norms.

DESCENT OF A BROKEN MAN

These societies expanded down the Nile River. However, they also expanded into Egyptian territory. Egypt conquered Nubian territories during different eras. However, relations between the two peoples also showed peaceful cultural interchange and cooperation, including mixed marriages," I continued.

The excitement in my voice filled the room and my broad natural smile created tension on my face. The sound of the strokes along the chalkboard evoked a rhythm of pleasure within me. The students, on the other hand, did not share my enthusiasm with the accomplishments of the ancient Nubian civilization. Some stared at the walls with disinterest, held conversations with each other, or entertained themselves with free hand notebook illustrations. My stomach boiled with annoyance as I took their disrespect personally. If I was a teacher who knew how to connect with people and managed to be popular with the kids, I would have their attention. However, there *was* a way to get some enthusiasm from them, and I wanted to shock them a little.

"In order to have these mixed marriages in that time, a shared religion was involved. Nubians also worshiped Horus, which is where the story of Jesus originated," I said with specific intention, my heart racing.

"Wait. Hold up, bruh! You tryna tell us Jesus ain't real?" a student replied, obviously unhappy.

"That's not what I'm saying, Devon. I'm saying that these ancient civilizations were not as unevolved as you were led to believe. Most had advanced technology that we still haven't figured out. Like the Gaza pyramids, for example. They weren't tombs like most believed; they were used for other purposes, possibly to harness energy. And most of the religions today share the same origin stories of these ancient civilizations, such as Horus and Jesus."

"Hold up, Mr. C. I dunno what you are talkin' about, but Jesus is the one true savior," a student belted out. "He is the one who sacrificed for our sins and saved us from judgment!"

"Okay," I replied. "Let's look at that for a moment. The Egyptian god Horus is said to be born from a virgin and is known for sacrificing himself for the sins of others. Sound familiar? Christianity is also known for duplicating stories from other religions, and also changing the stories to fit the agenda of the powers that be. Look at King James. King James the First wanted a new translation of the Bible to solidify his power and prove his own supremacy."

"No!" another student yelled out in disgust. "You will not

21

blaspheme! What are you talking about? No primitive civilization had the knowledge and intelligence to build these things or know of the one true God," Devon interjected.

As I listened to my students say the phrase one true God, it irritated me. With everything I had learned on religion and history, I admit my faith lacked a bit, but his words were cringeworthy.

"That's not accurate," I replied. "These civilizations were far from primitive and it is fact that people implemented certain aspects of Christianity in order to get the masses to follow them and maintain power. I'm not bashing your religion or anyone else's here; I'm just establishing the capabilities of these civilizations and the sophistication of their religious beliefs. We are still tapping into these sources today. Let's look at Christmas, for example. Christmas has lots of Pagan roots. Not Pagan as in devil worship, but as in secular. First, no one knows when Jesus was actually born. Early Christians wanted to convert Pagans into Christianity, so they used certain celebratory aspects of Paganism. The Christmas tree was a German invention from the 17th century. Christmas was also moved to the winter solace, so it could be celebrated during other Pagan celebrations. Gift giving wasn't practiced during Christmas until the 1800s, and was thought to be started by Queen Victoria," I lectured. "What you see today is not original. So, ask yourself, whose God is the real God? What happened to these people to make them want to worship a deity that is hardly known to us? What political powers were around that gave the people the results they prayed for in their worship? Studying religions with political power used by the Nubians and Persians, for example, can teach us a thing or two about power and sacrifice. They deserve our respect."

I glanced at the stunned faces among my students as the class bell chimed, breaking the deafening silence that claimed the class atmosphere.

"You are fucking crazy, Mr. C," a student yelled, laughing as he left the class.

I turned my back to scribble an assignment on the board, but by the time I had written *Read chapters 13 and 14 on the control of Egypt by the Nubians and prepare for testing next Monday,* someone threw a squeezable stress ball at the back of my head and most of the students had scurried from the classroom.

The ball caused me no physical pain, but the embarrassment was enough for me to avoid investigating the who-done-it and why. I just wanted the moment to pass.

DESCENT OF A BROKEN MAN

After I wrote the assignment and gave the last instructions to the class, I turned from the chalkboard and stared at the empty desks in front of me.

"Class dismissed."

CHAPTER FOUR

"Something isn't right."
—Detective Maor

Detective Nola Maor sat at her desk and skimmed through a pile of police reports when she overheard the frivolous conversations of her colleagues nearby.

The debates were juvenile and offensive toward minorities and women, but Maor found it easier to let some things slide for the purpose of her own peace within the boy's club. She often wondered if her older sister had it right by doing this job on the federal level. Thoughts of a more professional work environment, along with the necessary resources and manpower of the FBI that would keep pace with the activities of criminals was professionally appealing.

Maor's handheld police radio consistently cut through the exchanges in the office; the dispatcher requested patrol assistants with one violent call for service after another. The unending bombardment of alerts involving shootings, stabbings, assaults, and robberies were like desperate cries for help from a city near its breaking point.

Detective Maor enjoyed watching the engaging lifestyles of her fellow detectives. However, she seldom indulged in the invites to the parties and barbeques, but admired the carefree and sociable attitude of those who wore the badge.

Listening to the bustling laughter of her fellow detectives in the room, Maor marveled at how easily social engagement came to some of them. The smile on her face grew as she overheard their conversations allowing her to be a part of the comradery without the engagement.

Maor knew plenty of people, but she no longer concerned herself in cultivating any relationships, romantic or otherwise. Her sole interest was her job and making a difference in the city she loved, New Orleans. Past relationships were just that— the past— and that was where she preferred to leave them. Trust did not come easily to Maor. Life events had robbed her of the ability to trust, and as a result, there were only a few individuals left in her twenty-two years old life and career where the term trust still applied.

"Hey, Maor," a voice called out from across the room.

The portly detective wore a large grin and his cheeks were the color of a bright red rose.

Detective Maor always wondered if he had a fake white beard stashed somewhere at home waiting for the festive holidays.

"We goin' out for drinks tonight. You comin'?" he asked.

The offer was an enticing one that would give the detective a chance to decompress from the tall pile of unsolved homicide case files spread across her desk, all accumulated faster than she could solve them. Maor preferred not to drink alone again tonight, but she could not in good conscience lose focus.

"102 to 1153," the radio on her desk blared, interrupting her thoughts.

"1153 to 102, go ahead," Detective Maor replied.

"Go to Channel 3, please," the police officer on the other end responded.

"Maor, we have a 29S over here on the corner of Saint Ann St. and N. Prieur St. Something doesn't look right about it. Do you want to come out and take a look?"

"Yes," Detective Maor answered. "I'll be there in 5 minutes."

Typical, she thought to herself. *It would not be a day in the First Precinct without a dead body, suicide or not.*

"Sorry, boys. Looks like I'll be a little busy tonight. I'm sure you'll find another woman's reputation to ruin," she said to her colleagues with a smirk on her face.

The room erupted into laughter as Maor stood from her desk.

"I'm not interested in seeing anyone lose their life, but this city doesn't need another homicide. Hey, Serge, I'm headed out to Saint Ann St.. It may be a straightforward suicide like it is classified, but I'm going to check it out. Besides, the uniform on scene thinks something is off."

"10-4, Nola. Keep me posted," the Sergeant's raspy voice yelled from the office.

"Hey, Maor, if you wrap that scene up early, meet us down on Frenchmen St. and have some drinks with us. We want the departments poster child in our company. Wait, are you old enough to drink?" The portly detective laughed again.

"You're an asshole, Lapowski," she replied.

Maor was the youngest detective on the force, and joined the police department as soon as the law allowed her to carry a firearm as a law enforcement officer. It didn't take long for her to make an impression on the leadership, given her fiery personality and impressive intelligence. It helped to have the highest solve rate in the city as well.

As she grabbed her green note pad and clipped her handheld radio onto her waistband, Detective Maor left the bullpen office. Dressed professionally, her army boots thumped against the tile floor. Maor exited the police station and jumped into her unmarked city vehicle.

The humidity of the overheated spring season made Maor rethink her black slacks and blue long-sleeved blouse. Perspiration trickled down her forehead and Maor took a sip of water from the bottle in her car. She rolled the windows down to get a feel for the night and gauge the mood of the city. The sound of music in the neighborhoods, parties, couples arguing, and basketball games made sense to her. She never expected silence, even at night.

Maor pulled up on the corner of Saint Ann St. and North Prieur. Plastic and glass crackled under her tires as she parked. The remnants of empty drug vials and makeshift crack pipes were scattered in the street; anything goes in the city.

The purple and black shotgun home on the corner, designed by Voodoo practitioners, had been under renovation for a while, but it now had an armed police officer on the front porch. A small crowd of nosey citizens had gathered behind the crime scene tape set up by the other primary officers on scene. The idea of death inside the dark-colored residence triggered some uneasiness from the stereotypical nonsense rumored about the Voodoo religion.

Maor loved horror movies, but some of her own uneasiness came from those typical movie tropes hinted at in reality.

"Ugh! How many times have I seen houses like this in ghost movies? Still, something is off," she said, staring at the reaction of the crowd gathered in the street.

Some gaped and covered their mouths in disbelief, and others hung and shook their heads with grief. There was more of a sense of loss here than the normal morbid curiosity of the public gathered at a crime scene. She exited her vehicle with a sense of urgency and hurried to the two officers already on scene.

"What do we have, guys?"

"Looks like a self-inflicted gunshot wound to the head, but there is some weird voodoo shit going on in there," the officer Anderson replied.

He led the way into the house, while his partner waited outside.

Detective Maor noticed the faded uniform he wore, no doubt from the many years of wash and wear, along with his salt and pepper hair. She considered it a badge of honor for him. It showed his longevity in a thankless job that took a lot of guts to do every day, if it's done properly. Maor didn't know the officer well, but she appreciated the admirable work he had done over the years. Because of that, she trusted his instincts.

As Detective Maor walked through the door of the shotgun home, a familiar stench hit her like a brick wall, and caused her to turn her head and place her finger under her nose as her eyes watered.

"Damn it. You never get used to that smell," she whispered.

A bloodied, swollen body was on the floor as she entered.

"It looks like he kneeled here when he shot himself. There are no chairs near him and the spray on the wall is low as well," officer Anderson said.

Maor examined the adult black male lying on his side in the middle of the living room floor, with a snub nose .38 caliber revolver in his hand, and a massive pool of blood staining the refurbished hardwood floor. She kneeled closer to the body and observed the gunpowder burns on his temple. The cheap, tan-colored slacks with the African print patterned shirt didn't signal wealth to her, more like something thrown together because of the clashing nature.

Detective Maor circled the small living room a couple feet away from the body, and as she took in her surroundings, she focused on the obscure details of the scene. However, the details didn't add up as she stared at her feet.

"Uh oh, guys. She's doing that thing again," the veteran officer whispered to one of his less experienced colleagues.

"Something isn't right here. This is a smaller caliber handgun, so there is a 75% chance the gun would not still be in his hand if he were kneeling in this spot," she pointed out. "Don't get me wrong, Officer;

that's not that high of a percentage, but it's high enough. Plus, his finger is still on the trigger."

"Nola, why do you stare at your shoes at crime scenes?" the officer asked.

"It's something me and my sister do when we are thinking. It helps us focus. We like to call it our superpower," Detective Maor jested. "The technical answer is hyperthymesia. It makes us pretty good at remembering details."

"Hyperthy—what? Whatever it is, it works for you," the officer replied.

Detective Maor looked up and continued to pace around the body. She stopped at the long narrow hallway that led from the living room to the rear of the house.

In New Orleans, shotgun homes were plentiful, and they got their name from the straight-line architecture. If you stood at the front of the home, you would be able to look down the open hallway and see the back of the house or shoot a shotgun from front to back.

As Maor strolled down the hall, she tutted at the darkness of the house with annoyance.

"Why are cops always apprehensive about turning on the lights at an indoor crime scene?" Detective Maor complained, feeling an uneasiness in the pit of her stomach.

When she reached the end of the hallway and entered the kitchen, her eyes widened at the gruesome sight, and she gagged at the stench from the rotten flesh that filled the room.

Dozens of half-melted candles were scattered about the table and countertop, and the walls were covered with blood spatter. Several severed chicken heads lay on the kitchen table, but the hand-painted message soaked in blood on the nearby wall caught her attention the most.

"*False god,*" she read as goosebumps raised on her arms. "Must have been in a rush; sloppy work."

The floorboards creaked behind Maor and she glanced over her shoulder.

"I see you've found the victim's kitchen," Anderson said. "This was why I wasn't sure about the scene. According to some folks in the neighborhood, everyone loved this guy. He kept a low profile, and the chicken heads were apparently his way of bringing good fortune to the people who came to him for help. Most of the people that came to him knew the chicken head thing was just for show, but they swear that whatever else was involved in his ritual worked. No one knows anything about any thugs from the project or anywhere else in the city that may have had a problem with him."

"I see," Maor replied. "I don't suppose any of them saw anyone suspicious come to visit our community man in the past few days?"

"No. No one saw anything. You know how it goes, Detective," he said.

"Thank you, Officer. When the crime lab gets here, make sure they work the scene from the front of the house to the back. We've had enough people walking through here today."

As the officer turned and walked away, Detective Maor noticed a square hole the size of a softball cut into the adjacent dry wall above the kitchen counter. White powder adorned the jagged edges of the hole, and the debris in front of it was fresh as if it were recently cut. Maor examined the hole a little closer with the flashlight she pulled from her rear pocket and illuminated the inside of the hole. She spotted a piece of sky-blue colored plastic inside the void.

Detective Maor grabbed the object and instantly recognized the shape of it; something she had held in her hand many times in her youth.

"Figures," she mumbled. "Of course, it's a rosary."

The sight of it filled her with anger and a feeling of loss that had lingered within her for a long time after being raised as a Catholic for too many years and living a devoted lifestyle.

"What a waste of time," she said.

Her flashlight illuminated another object inside, and Maor reached in again to pull out a piece of white folded paper.

Her instincts told her that whatever information the note contained, it would only confirm what she already thought.

Maor unfolded the paper. Her hands trembled and she hoped she would be proven wrong.

'One True God,' the note read. She closed her eyes and took a deep breath as she shook her head.

Maor pressed a button on her radio and spoke into it. "1153 to dispatch."

"Go 'head, 1153," a voice replied.

"Let's go ahead and change this to a homicide signal 30S. How long until the crime lab arrives?"

"They are working another 30S currently. It's about a 60-minute wait," the dispatcher replied.

Maor sighed. "10-4, I'll notify the Lieutenant."

"10-4, ma'am."

Maor looked around the room and noticed the surrounding insanity, and she exhaled at the thought of another religious monster out there.

"Another zealot? I don't want to deal with this. I don't want to deal with you. God, I left you behind for a reason," Maor whispered, her head shook in disgust.

CHAPTER FIVE

"James, you're awfully quiet as usual."
—Mr. Lee

The chairs that surrounded the outdated and worn table in the faculty lounge were uncomfortable, common knowledge among the faculty, but that didn't matter. I would rather sit in the uncomfortable chairs to read my research notes than on the ratty brown couch in the corner with assorted tears and unknown stains. Rumors of staff affairs always hinted at what those stains could be; typical of the school district. I wondered if the schools in the more affluent parts of town had these issues.

I leaned on my fist as I read over my notes at the large break table and half listened to my coworkers around me. Their conversations seemed interesting, but I always tried to tune them out and appear as focused on my work as possible for fear they may try to include me. The thought of conversing in a group gave me anxiety, especially as I had overheard both the English and Civics teachers gossiping about the lecture I had given in class on Christianity. Their smirks and snickers solidified that I should steer clear of their conversation.

"James, you're awfully quiet as usual," Mr. Lee said, sitting across from me at the table. "Something bugging you today?"

"Mr. Lee, man, how is it going today, sir?" I said, cheery and upbeat. "Just taking the time to go over some of my research. Still trying to get published and teach people some things. I have to keep my nose in these books."

Mr. Lee was the ninth-grade science teacher and always engaged with me as if we were long-time friends. Although my nerves often got the better of me, socializing with Mr. Lee helped me to appear as socially normal as possible in the workplace.

"Research, huh? I thought the science guys were the nerds of the school," Lee joked, noticing my fidgety fingers.

I cracked a weak smile at Lee's joke, and he eyed me with suspicion.

"James, when are we going to hang out, man? We can go get some drinks and you can help me pick up a lady or two. It would help to have another handsome fella around," Mr. Lee said.

"Mr. Lee, we aren't going anywhere, unless you shave that crusty beard you have sitting on your face."

"What you mean, *crusty?*" he protested with laughter, stroking its uneven growth. "This is my signature look! The ladies love the wild salt and pepper mane."

"Man, I have to see this live and up close. I could use the laugh. We definitely have to hit up a bar or two, Mr. Lee," I said, absent of a smile.

"You sure you're all right, James? The wife riding you pretty hard at home? You seem down in the dumps today but lay off your fingernails before there is nothing left but blood and tissue," Lee said with a grin.

"Yeah, you're right, Lee," I admitted. "I just... you ever had this deep feeling of despair you couldn't shake, or just couldn't..."

"What the hell are you talking about, James? You are a black man in America. There is no time for despair. Whatever you are going through, we've all been through it. Don't be weak. It'll pass," said Mr. Lee.

"That's not what I'm talking about," I said coldly, returning to my notes.

But as I tried to refocus, the faculty lounge door swung open. Dr. Wilson entered the room and found me with her cold tense eyes.

"Mr. Corbin, I need to see you in my office. Immediately!" she yelled.

I looked up to see Dr. Wilson's pursed lips and furrowed eyebrows, a sight all too familiar.

"On my way, Dr. Wilson," I mumbled.

My colleagues stared at me across the room, as I placed my notebook back into my briefcase and followed Dr. Wilson.

What now? I thought.

DESCENT OF A BROKEN MAN

The moment I stepped into Dr. Wilson's office, I realized how frequently I had been there and sat in the guest chair before her desk. Files covered every surface and framed accomplishments of her past, both academic and philanthropic, adored the walls. Her award for developing The Fresh Look program caught my eye every time I entered the office; a program that allowed the school district to become more financially efficient so we could purchase more books and equipment to upgrade facilities.

However, her so called noble gesture to the school didn't lessen the fact that this woman criticized me at every opportunity.

"Mr. Corbin, do you know how much trouble you have caused me? Your offensive behavior regarding religion in your lecture is causing an influx of calls from angry parents. This is unacceptable! I need you to understand that you are a history teacher, not a philosophy professor. You are hanging by a thread here; I have no quarrels about firing you and hiring a history teacher who cooperates and stays within the lesson plan. Do you understand?" Dr. Wilson warned, glowering over her glasses.

"Yes, Dr. Wilson, but..."

"No buts!" Wilson yelled. "You seem to think you are more than what you are, but you are nothing but a simple high school history teacher, and an average one at that. You have not shown the talent *or* the focus to be anything more. Do yourself a favor and keep the topics nice and boring. Regurgitate the dates of events like you are supposed to do and answer your students' questions without offending them. Otherwise, you will find yourself exactly what you teach — history. Do we understand each other?"

"Yes, Dr. Wilson," I replied through gritted teeth, gripping the arms of the chair.

My knuckles turned pale and my jaw ached from clenching it.

I knew I had a chance to be more than a history teacher when Dr. Wilson stole my program presentation for The Fresh Look program and passed it off as her own to the school board, but I struggled to find the guts and self-worth to stand up for myself.

"You are dismissed, Mr. Corbin," she finished.

I stood with haste and exited the room, slamming the door behind me. The vibration caused one of the dozen frames to crash to the floor, but I didn't care.

"What a bitch!" I hissed on the other side of the door, but somehow Dr. Wilson heard me.

"Mr. Corbin!" Dr. Wilson barked, attempting to gain my attention.

I rushed from the office area and toward the parking lot as the bell sounded in the background.

Dr. Wilson's words pissed me off the more I thought about what she said, and her venomous words struck every insecurity I had. Not worthy of better things. Inadequate. Not good enough. Blood raced through my veins and I gripped the cracked leather steering wheel tighter.

As I reflected on the day during my drive, I could feel how alone life's journey had become. As Mr. Lee reminded me, life was hard enough as a black man in America, being immediately judged when I walked into a room. *I can't win*, I thought. Car horns blared around me as I sped through the residential streets.

"Slow down, asshole!" a driver yelled in my direction.

My breathing calmed the further I drove from the school and the closer I got to my home and my wife. Just the thought of being around Candace had a calming effect. I could hear the words she had spoken so often early on in our marriage.

"All you can be is yourself, James," she would say. Although, she doesn't say it much anymore.

It made sense being someone else every day to avoid the traps America has for black men. It's taken its toll and blurred the lines of who I'm supposed to be, I thought.

I parked in the driveway of my home and took a deep breath. My arms fell from the steering wheel to my sides. My head once again hit the back of the head rest as I looked at the large window in front. I hoped Candace was in a good mood. The sight of the window made me reflect on our early years in our marriage and how close we were. The smile on her face when she saw the three large panel windows and spacious porch that would provide an unobstructed view into our neighborhood and allowed us to appreciate the sights of the city, sometimes the random second-line that would make its way down our street. The smile on Candace's face when she laid her eyes upon the house made price haggling a little tougher, but I wanted to make her content, so I paid a little more for it.

Candace was always my calming force. The moments we had shared since the day of our wedding over the last five years have been a rollercoaster, but they have only made me appreciate Candace more. My love ran deeper for her than I could have ever imagined. However, these days, I wasn't convinced the feeling was mutual.

I quickly popped my head up again. I forced myself from another daydream before I left the solitude of my car. The thought of holding Candace after such a rough day gave me a bit of comfort, but when I peered through the three-panel window and spotted her disappointed scowl, my heart dropped.

My stomach twisted into a knot and my legs weakened, but I couldn't stay in the car all night and avoid her obvious discontent.

"I don't know what's wrong, but I do not feel like dealing with any more shit after the day I've had," I said. As I slammed my car door and approached the house, I wondered what more could possibly go wrong.

"Hello, baby," I greeted her. "How was your day?"

"Fine," Candace said with a blunt tone. An awkward silence stood between us as if we were situated in two different rooms.

After a long moment, Candace finally turned to face me.

"I'm sick of your shit, James! I expected more from you. I'm not interested in living an average, boring life. We've been married for five years, James, and you have accomplished nothing but being a broke ass high school history teacher. All you do is research and write, but nothing happens. It takes all of your time!" Candace shouted as tears swamped her eyes. "You no longer show me the attention I deserve, and you have no money to occupy my time on top of it. What good are you? You sometimes spend days at a time in bed. You don't want to move. You don't want to eat. How long do I have to wait around for you?"

Candace's demeanor calmed, but the smeared mascara continued to roll down her cheeks with her tears.

I froze with shock as I listened to the harsh words that poured from my wife's mouth. "Candace, I..."

"You are a loser, James. Marrying you was a mistake and I deserve better than this," she barked. "I'm better than you and I need to leave now if I want to have any chance at a good life!"

Candace stood from the black sofa and gave me a poisonous glare, but I looked away from her gaze and focused on the luggage a few feet away from her.

"Do you hear me, James?" she yelled. "I'm leaving. Don't call me. I'll have a lawyer contact you. I want nothing from you. You don't have shit, anyway!"

Candace left our house and slammed the front door behind her, causing my body to jerk. I always thought I'd chase after her if our marriage came to this, but all I could do was freeze and watch the love of my life jump into her red sports car and thunder away with screeching tires.

My chest tightened as I gasped for air, and my gut ripped apart with pain. I dropped my briefcase with devastation, and it thumped into the hardwood floor. Slow, deep breaths prevented another painful anxiety attack and I continued to stare at the door. My legs felt heavy, as if they were planted into the floor.

As the shock from Candace's blow wore off, I could finally speak.

"I guess I have work to do," I mumbled, my voice breaking.

I headed to my home office with heavy reluctance and intended to focus on the last thing I had left in life — my research.

CHAPTER SIX

"The devil is in the details."
—Detective Maor

Detective Maor was not fond of old wives' fables. She couldn't remember how often she had heard the tale of hot weather contributing to more violence. Although she had never looked at any hard data to support that, the previous week had done nothing but convince her that this particular myth was probable. The unusually warm spring had made itself prevalent, and the city's body count increased right along with it.

"Hey, Maor! You still working on the Voodoo king case?" Lapowski yelled from across the bullpen office. "Who knew he would have company? What's that, four bodies now? God bless 'em. I hope they take out all those mumbo jumbo voodoo folk!"

His oversized belly bounced as he chuckled at his own clever comment. The surrounding detectives erupted into laughter, sharing the crass sense of humor.

Lapowski often slumped behind his desk with a roast beef po-boy and gave the other detectives a hard time; after that, he wasn't much use. Most of the detectives knew he never cared about the lives of the people he swore to protect, and this truth started to grate on Maor.

"Lapowski, your remarks are unbecoming of the badge. Shut your pie hole, put on a clean shirt, and clear a case!" Maor snapped, even though Lapowski had a point about the similarities in victims.

Over the past month, Detective Maor had acquired three additional murder cases with a note saying, '*One True God*' and a blue plastic rosary left somewhere on the scene. Lapowski was wrong, however, about Voodoo being in the center of it all. Not all of the victims were Voodoo practitioners. One was a Muslim, another was Jewish, and all four were men, but she wouldn't expect someone like Lapowski to worry about the details.

The last thing this city needs is a serial killer hell bent on teaching some sort of religious lesson, she thought.

"Detective Maor, come into my office, please," her sergeant's voice called out from the only other room connected to the cubicle-style seating area the detectives shared.

Detective Sergeant Pine generally stayed in his office and concerned himself only with the crime patterns and repeat offenders in the First Precinct.

Detective Maor walked into his smoke-filled office and anticipated another professional conversation, like the ones she had enjoyed many times before about the ins and outs of the police department and strategies the homicide detectives could use to clear more cases. Every now and then, the conversation would touch on the lack of significant others in their lives, but nothing more. Pine was one of the few who could match Maor's dedication to make a real change in the job, no doubt because of the sense of duty he developed after twenty-five years in the military.

"Have a seat, Detective. Lapowski is an asshole, isn't he?" Sergeant Pine asked, looking down at a file on his desk.

Detective Maor sat across from him and smirked. "Yes. Yes, he is, Serge."

"You haven't been doing this job long, but Lapowski is what you get when you lose your sense of duty and become jaded about the people you swore to protect. Don't let me see that happen to you. You got me?"

"Yeah, Serge. I get it," Maor replied.

"I've been reading the reports, Maor. I think what we have on our hands here is pretty obvious, but I want to hear it from that big brain of yours."

"Serge, the commonalities of each case show that these victims were attacked by the same perpetrator," Maor explained. "All of them were shot in the head by a .38 caliber handgun while kneeling, most likely a snub-nosed revolver like the one found on the first scene, and their hands were bound by duct tape, which was a little different from the first. I think he evolved a little since Saint. Ann St. Each scene also had a handwritten note and a light blue rosary. There were no signs of forced entry at any of the residences, and nothing was taken from the homes. Each of the bodies were found in the living areas near the front door."

"Why the living rooms?" Sergeant Pine asked.

"I'm not sure if it is a matter of convenience or if it means something, but whoever killed the victims knew them, Sergeant."

"Then, of course, the next question is who do all —"

"Whom do all the victims know so well they would allow them into their homes?" Detective Maor interrupted.

The sound of laughter erupted from outside the office, making it difficult to concentrate. Maor closed her eyes and refocused on each scene in her mind.

"The kills are clean, and the victims begged for their lives, Serge. I wonder what your God would think of that?" Maor whispered to herself.

"Excuse me, Detective? Don't get too familiar. And don't be an asshole like Lapowski," Sergeant Pine interjected.

Maor leaned back in her chair. The smell of the smoke turned her stomach and she subtly rolled her eyes at the clear lack of respect for the non-smokers on the team.

"I was raised Catholic. My family was pretty dedicated, but it turned sour for me. I meant no offense. Anyway, the rosary, Serge, it's part of the Catholic religion, but none of the victims were Catholic. My guess is that the victims are being punished; it's not retribution."

"Find this creep, Maor. Do what you do best. Keep me updated," Sergeant Pine said.

Detective Maor nodded, and her stomach knotted with anxiety as she left his office.

"Later, boys," she said as she headed for the main entrance, trying to ignore the odor of sweat and stale cigarettes. "Make sure you guys bathe tonight. I don't want to smell this stench tomorrow."

They laughed and wished her a good night, but their overwhelming guffaws were a not-so-subtle reminder of her limited acceptance into the boys' club.

Maor strolled out of the station into the humid night, and she listened to the police sirens in the distance.

After getting into her city-issued police car, she strapped on her seatbelt and adjusted her mirrors. She pulled out of the station; the details and whys of her cases nagged at her. All the moving parts and witness interviews bounced around her head like pieces to a puzzle.

"The devil is in the details," she said, pressing her foot on the gas pedal.

Three different religions, no forced entry, execution style? No food was found on any of the scenes. No alcohol. No cigarettes. Not even a glass of water to suggest the hosting of company.

The drive to the Westbank of the city always flew by, though Detective Maor had a heavy foot behind the wheel. She pulled into her assigned space in the community parking lot of her apartment complex, and the security light along the stairwell illuminated her way up the stairs to her second-floor apartment. She glanced over her shoulder and remained cautious of her surroundings all the way up the stairs, but thankfully, no one emerged from the darkness.

As Maor opened the front door, she turned on the lights and grabbed the mail from the floor. Nothing eventful, just a newsletter from her Catholic church welcoming the new Deacon.

Detective Maor didn't know why she continued to get solicitations from the church she had not attended in years, but out of curiosity she read the newsletter.

The new Deacon, Nicholas Bianchi, comes from Rome, Italy, and has been an active participant in the community since moving to New Orleans. He believes God loves all, regardless of economic status, race, gender, nonbelievers, and even those who worship false gods. His goal is to help New Orleans reduce its crime through humanitarian efforts.

"Maybe there is hope for the church after all. Not a bad looking man either." Maor scoffed and rolled her eyes, hearing herself.

Not a chance, she thought. *Not for the church. New Orleans doesn't need the church; it needs jobs.*

Maor grabbed the leftover salad from her refrigerator and the frosted bottle of vodka from her freezer and poured herself a robust amount in a drinking glass. A quick swallow pushed her to exhale as she relaxed her shoulders and lowered her head, pouring more, as she replaced what she had already drank. Glass in hand, Maor walked toward her impressive bookcase near her couch and read over the titles. Her finger dragged across the seam of each book as she read through in search for the resource she looked for. As Maor took another sip, her finger stopped at the green hardcover book she hoped would provide more insight into the psycho she was dealing with.

"I didn't think you would be anything more than a curiosity," she said as she read the front cover. *A Guide to History's Notorious Religious Zealots.*

Maor took the book and bottle and sat at the wooden desk in her living room. She powered on her computer and poured herself a little more vodka as she waited for the internet to load properly. Her face winced at the annoyance of the erratic dings and pings of the dial up internet tapping into the phone lines. The sound was only overtaken by the ring of her cell phone.

"Hello."

"Hey, girl. What are you doing?" the energetic voice on the other end of the phone asked.

"Janice? Hey, girl. I didn't expect to hear from you this time of the night."

"Yeah, it's been a few days since I talked to you and I wanted to check in. How's my baby sister?" she asked.

"I'm good. Work keeps me plenty busy. You know how home is. Plus, it looks like I've got something pretty interesting going on now," Maor replied.

"Interesting? By interesting, I hope you mean a man?"

"Damn it! No, Janice. I don't have time for a man and I'm not interested in making time right now either."

"Nola, you can't make your job your life. You have to have balance, sweetie. We are both in law enforcement and I understand the challenges of the department you work for, but you can't do it all yourself. You can't save everyone, Nola."

"I know, Janice. It looks like we may have a serial killer on the loose. Someone like Father Williams."

"Oh my God. Nola, are you sure?"

"I'm sure, Janice. This nut job is leaving rosaries and a note that reads *One True God* at every scene."

"Jesus. Look, Nola, I know you are more than capable, but if you need the help of the Feds, just give me a call and I'll make it happen. I'm right here in Nashville and I can have a team there in no time."

"Thanks, girl, but I don't need the FBI for this. I can handle it. On another note, how are you and the hubby?"

"We are good. Well, actually, we are great. A little surprise. Nola, I'm pregnant."

"What? Oh my God! Congrats, Janice! I'm going to be an Auntie? I'm so excited!"

"Look, I'm headed into the house. I haven't told him yet. Seriously, Nola, if you need my help with this case, just call me. I love you, little sis."

"I love you too, Janice. Talk to you soon."

After talking with Janice, Maor took a few bites of her salad, and refocused as she typed the names of the victims into the search engine with the hope of discovering more details about their deaths.

None of them had arrest records or previous convictions; they all played a large role in helping their communities through good works, charitable events, and mentoring children abandoned by society. As a result, none of these men had any known enemies.

As Maor scrolled through the search results, she recognized one of the victims in a news report about a religious mentoring program.

Local religious leaders come together to develop mentoring program for New Orleans youth, the headline read.

Upon clicking the link, a picture popped up of six men. Four of the men were victims, posing in front of the site of the new mentoring headquarters, Serving Hope and Purpose Every Day. S.H.A.P.E. for short. Their bright smiles suggested they were happy with their accomplishment, but Maor's frown deepened, and her eyes widened.

"These men were partners," Maor said with surprise.

As she searched deeper into the details of this mentoring program, a thunderous storm roared outside and heavy raindrops pounded the windows of her apartment. Most people would be alarmed or fascinated by the wild weather, but its ferocity only helped Maor focus.

She stared at the photograph of the S.H.A.P.E. partners with dipped eyebrows, and her curiosity made her wonder how people with such different backgrounds found each other. Her eyes widened at a familiar name listed under the picture and her head slightly tilted at his face.

"I just saw him. That name. That face... Nicholas Bianchi. This has nothing to do with money," she concluded. "There is more at play here. It's going to be a long night."

CHAPTER SEVEN

"Things come and things go. This place is just a gateway."
—Priestess Nadia

The stomach pains distracted me from the task at hand, but thankfully, the pain also distracted my mind from the heart piercing words of my wife that echoed in my head.

Should I go after her? I thought as I paced my office; my hands trembled and my eyes were red. *No. I always tried to be a good husband, but how could I have given her the life she wanted if I didn't make a name for myself?*

I slid down to the floor as my chest constricted and stared at the collection of papers on my desk, but the thought of how far I was from reaching my goals made me feel worse.

How could she not see my plans, my effort? The research would lead to publication, professorship, speaking engagements, and book publications. More money for her to live in comfort.

My breathing became shallow and erratic, and the room spun. My sight blurred, and I gasped for every ounce of air I could inhale.

I remembered what to do from so many times before, so I tilted my head back and took several deep breaths to the count of ten, silently praying to a God I didn't necessarily have faith in.

"Please. Please, God. I hate these," I mumbled, focusing on my slow breaths.

Several moments passed, and I slowly stood to my feet again with weak muscles and my hands braced against the desk. My legs were weak, and I could barely stand, emotionally drained on top of everything that had happened that day. I could practically hear my wife yelling the words, "man up" at me as she had so many times before. I always hated that phrase; it was dismissive and only trivialized the person's struggle.

Candace may be right, though. Black men didn't see shrinks, and there was no way I would take any meds. I would be a laughingstock and lose what little respect I had from people, I thought.

I hobbled to the cracked leather chair behind the desk and slumped into it with a heavy sigh.

"Focus, James. You can do this. It's the only road you have left," I said to myself, as I slid my papers aside and concentrated on the large journal underneath the papers.

In an attempt to put my distressing day behind me, I read over my research notes about Ancient Persia's religious practices and deities. Persia's history often bored others, but the strength of their culture throughout history intrigued me. I knew my choice of highlighting the Persian Empire was problematic, even at the Historian Conference I attended a few weeks ago.

The relatively modest sized auditorium was filled with some of the region's most brilliant academic historians, publishers, and college instructors. The conference provided professional development through an abundance of sessions, plenaries, and workshops, and I did my best to attend every year.

"Hello, Dean Henton. Glad to see you made it again this year," I said.

"James! It's good to see you. Glad you could make it again this year as well. How is life at Robert E. Lee High School?" Dean Henton said as he tugged on the front edges of his sport coat.

For the time I had known Dean Henton, he had always worn that sport coat. I only saw him in a professional environment such as these conferences, but it didn't matter the weather; he always had on that coat.

"Things are going well. I'm not the Dean of the History department at a major university or anything, but things are still going well. I have some research I'm finishing up that I think is unique and groundbreaking enough to get me that publication."

"James, I see you are still plugging away. You just won't give up, will you? You do know that it's okay to be a high school history teacher, don't you?"

"I think this is different, Dean. I've found some things about

DESCENT OF A BROKEN MAN

ancient Persia that will change everything. I just need to find a little more evidence."

"Okay, I'll play along. What are your findings? This better be good, James."

"Oh, it's very good. As we know, the Persian Empire remained in power for centuries in what is now modern-day Iran, due to the enduring success of the Iron Age Dynasty – a global hub of culture, religion, science, art, and technology."

"Jesus... James, I'm bored already. If you are going to recite historical facts everyone in this building already knows, except for the hotdog vendor, then I see why you've failed," the Dean smiled as he waved at a colleague a few feet away.

I exhaled deeply as I closed my eyes and refocused.

"Well, the facts I've uncovered that make this interesting are what was harder to find. Persia was one of the earlier civilizations to capitalize off the dark arts to push themselves forward, or even backwards, depending on the person wielding the power. However, no one ever found documentation to prove that Persia was involved in the dark arts...until now," I said as I grinned.

The Dean's eyes darted back in my direction. "You have documented evidence of this? Where did you find it?"

"Persia was shaped by a religion called Zoroastrianism, the first recorded religion with the belief of one god, Zoroaster, and also the same duality of most religions today, correct? Well, it came from a collection of Zoroastrian religious scriptures known as the Avesta. People believed that Zoroaster had a divine vision of a consuming light after his family surrounding him gave him an overwhelming feeling of gratefulness. In this vision, Zoroaster was spoken to by the god of light and fire, Ahura Mazda, who showed a symbol that he proceeded to burn into his forehead."

"I'm familiar with the Zoroastrian religion and the Avesta. It's already documented. As a matter of fact, James, many cultures have religious fairytales just like it. What about the evidence of the actual occurrences?" His tone was in step with his impatience.

"It was the symbols," I replied as I peeled my cuticles. "One early Persian text led to the only supposed quote by Ahura Mazda: 'Grace is your reward for spiritual light. Go forward and spread my word and you will continue to be rewarded. Stay away from the internal darkness; it will lead you to blood and death.'

"The only connection located was during the time of James Cyrus the Great, founder of the Achaemenid Persian Empire, and

47

known as a tolerant, loving ruler, who propelled Zoroastrianism and the worship of Ahura Mazda to the forefront of Persian civilization. Cyrus placed the symbol of Ahura Mazda on all public buildings and temples as a tribute to him. His priestess performed miracles for those who worshiped him and brought protection and favor over Persia."

"I don't know, James. That's pretty weak. I wouldn't print it. It's not enough. Keep digging. I'm sure you'll find the missing pieces you need. It was nice seeing you again," Dean replied, with his hand on my shoulder.

That conference was the start of an eventful evening. The words of the Dean played over and over in my head that night. Although I had a great interest in ancient history as a whole, the religious aspects of Persia were the driving force behind my research and infatuation. The newly discovered, underlying influences of the occult had me hell-bent on proving the supernatural influence on faith-based, religious practices, and how it had always been the cause for some of the most amazing accomplishments, as well as many evil acts in world history.

However, the mistake I made was presenting the topic in academia. It had resulted in me being laughed out of the conference that night. It was fringe enough to have me doubt my own mental prowess at times, especially on my dark days.

"It'll be different this time. I kept digging, Dean, and I found it," I said to myself.

For the first time in years, I believed in this work, and a wave of excitement surged through me as I continued to read over the rest of my research and scribbles. The ability to prove that Zoroastrianism and deities from ancient Egypt helped to shape major Abrahamic religions, such as Judaism, Islam, and Christianity, would be enough to get the paper published, and proof of the use of the occult would be new enough to make a name for myself.

As the thunderous sky outside opened up and the rain pounded against my office window, I thanked the heavens for allowing me to find the old book I tightly clasped with both hands.

Before I found this book in Nadia's Voodoo shop, my research only brought more questions to fester with my drive to prove that the supernatural had a real influence on historical events. It often led to some disturbing readings, and some dark thoughts as well. The book showed me the symbol James Cyrus used. The symbol of Ahrua Mazda.

DESCENT OF A BROKEN MAN

Priestess Nadia's Voodoo Emporium, a non-traditional store in an old shotgun home, was in a small corner of New Orleans, miles from the tourist traps. Nadia, an older lady who collected rare supernatural antiquities and claimed to still practice Voodoo, became a good friend to me over the years.

She turned into one of the few people I could bare my soul to, even about the struggles inside me.

Although the sound of the rain outside calmed me, the book on my desk put me on edge as I thought more about the night it came into my possession.

When I left the conference on that late, dark night last week, exhaustion overwhelmed me after engaging in a two-hour long social discussion about religion with Dean Henton and a bunch of old white men who didn't rank high on my 'good time' list. I stuck out like a sore thumb. Still, networking would only help me in the future.

While I drove through the small town outside Orleans Parish, a majority white suburb of New Orleans, and headed home, a set of blue lights flashed behind me, signaling for me to pull over.

"Ah! Come on!" I complained, squinting my eyes as the blue lights reflected in my mirrors and blinded me. Easily the fourth time I had been pulled over in my trips through there.

With reluctance, I pulled over and rested my head on my hand, which tightly gripped the steering wheel.

The deputy whacked his baton against my driver's side window and shone his flashlight in my eyes when I rolled it down.

"What are you doing back here?" the deputy asked.

The stench of the late summer night and the unbathed law enforcement officer assaulted my nose immediately. The light from his torch shielded his face and name tag, so the tattooed Iron Cross on his forearm, the same Iron Cross used by the Nazis during World War II, was all I could see.

"Excuse me?" I replied.

"You heard me. Don't make me ask you again. It's too late for you to be back here."

"I didn't realize there was a curfew in Beauregard Parish," I snapped with incredulousness. *"You didn't have a reason to stop me. It's the same shit every time I come back here. The stares from people and the harassment from you police. I came here for a Religious History Conference at the Center. I'm not bothering anybody. If you didn't stop me, I'd be out of your shitty parish by now."*

"Religious history? Are you kiddin' me, nigger?" the deputy scoffed, his belly shaking as he laughed.

The officer's racist language made me grip the steering wheel so tight my knuckles turned white, and I glared directly into the brightness to try and get a good look at his face.

No matter how much I squinted, I still couldn't see him, so I reached for the door handle and scowled at the officer.

"What the fuck did you just call me?" I yelled, but before I could vacate my car, the officer pressed the steel barrel of his gun against my temple.

I froze and trembled with fear at the thought of losing my life by his hand. Nevertheless, a part of me wanted him to pull the trigger.

"Don't you fuckin' move, nigger," the officer ordered in a calm but firm manner. *"Put your hands back on that steering wheel and off the door handle. Tonight— tonight is your lucky night. I get off in twenty minutes and I don't feel like cleaning up your blood. So, leave my fuckin' parish, and leave the books and history for white men with brains."*

The officer struck me across the face with a forceful blow. A sharp pain followed throughout my lower jaw. The butt of his gun forced its way into my car, temporarily breaking the intense beam of intrusive light in my eyes, and that became the last thing I saw before the pain turned into a permanent distraction.

I touched my cheek and sped off without seeing the deputy's name or face, only that Iron Cross on his arm.

As I sped back into Orleans Parish and through the lower Ninth Ward, I decided to visit my old friend, Priestess Nadia. She had always been a reasonable voice for me, and at that point, I needed that reasonable voice to prevent me from making any rash decisions.

Light peered through her front window when I pulled up, and I smiled at her dark silhouette pottering about inside. It was late, but Nadia always told me that if the lights were on, she was open for business, so I left my car and strolled up the steps to her shotgun home.

DESCENT OF A BROKEN MAN

"Well, hello, James," her calm voice greeted me upon my entrance. "Hello, ma'am. Sorry I dropped by so late. How you feelin' tonight?" I asked with caution as my jaw throbbed with pain.

"Strong," she replied. "I've been waiting for you. I knew you would come by tonight. However, I don't have anything new for you to see, but feel free to look around. How is your research going? Are you close?"

Nadia's warm smile matched her voice and made me feel as though I were listening to soft jazz at the end of a rough night.

Her curly salt and pepper hair slipped out from under her red bandana, and her wooden cane supported the limp she had suffered from for as long as I could remember.

"Ma'am, have you ever felt provoked, down to your very soul? Have so much rage in you that it's hard to contain?" I asked, wincing at the sharp pain that surged through the left side of my jaw.

Nadia eyed me with sympathy, but she knew I had more to say, and let me continue to let everything out as the memory of the deputy's gun across my face flashed through my mind.

"I don't belong here. Why do these things keep happening to me? Isn't the depression enough?" I questioned, clenching my teeth. "Tonight, I felt a particular rage I have not felt before."

Nadia sighed. "James, the world owes you nothing. Not fairness. Not happiness. Not even love. Those are things you must find. Your purpose is to feed your spirit, not your flesh. Help your fellow man and indulge in the joys of life. I believe your heart is pure, James, but your depression has a hold on you that not even I can help you with. You need to seek a professional's help. Someone who can treat the sickness. That's what it is, James, a sickness that will only make it harder for you to deal with life's challenges."

"I hear you, Priestess," I said. "But shouldn't I do my best to reach my full potential while I'm here? Don't I at least owe that to myself? How can I help others if I feel worthless in the process? I just want to reach my full potential without the interference of—" I paused.

On a shelf in the far-left corner of the room, I noticed an ancient-looking book; something different to Nadia's usual antiques and rarities. Even from a distance, its spine and battered cover told me that it was worn and old.

"I thought you didn't have anything new, ma'am?" I asked.

"I don't," she said. "It appears something has found you."

I took a closer look and realized that I had never seen anything like this book before. The cover felt like an old animal's skin, and there were no titles, subtitles, or author's names on the front or back cover, just two triangular symbols. One of them had a black circle in the middle with a red drip hanging from it, and the other also had a black circle in the middle, but with an orange flame firing out the top.

I didn't recognize the former, but I instantly knew the latter to be the symbol of light from the Zoroastrian religion; the spirit mark of Ahura Mazda.

My insides swirled with a mixture of disbelief and excitement when I peeked inside and discovered that the book had been written or translated into modern English.

I turned to the Priestess. "Is it for sale?"

"No," she replied.

Nadia's expression had grown cold and emotionless, and her features had hardened.

"You know how my shop works, James. Things come and things go. This place is just a gateway," she told me in a somber tone. "The book is meant for you. I didn't bring it here. Yet, it was here for you. Take it and go. It appears there is something waiting for you in the near future. I pray it brings your spirit peace. Use it wisely."

Priestess Nadia sat back in her chair and looked away from me.

"Goodnight, Nadia. Honest and straightforward as usual. Thank you for everything," I said with a smile, and headed back to my car, completely oblivious to her stressed and worried tone of voice.

Maybe if I had paid closer attention to Nadia's worries that night, I would have had the guts to seek the help she told me I needed, regardless of what others thought. I didn't think showing that type of weakness would be a smart move as both a husband and an aspiring researcher and historian.

Shaken by the thunder rolling through the sky, I returned to the

DESCENT OF A BROKEN MAN

present, away from that painful night.

I opened the book with the intention of delving deeper into its text and exploring my passion further, but the unknown symbol with the red, faded drip distracted me. However, I decided to study it in more detail once I had a full understanding of Ahura Mazda.

Intrigued, I rubbed my thumb over the symbols' indentations on the cover and read the small inscription in the upper right corner of the inside page. Oddly enough, it was written in English but in a Vladimir Script type of handwriting. The script read *Book of Blood* in faded red ink. My heart thumped in anticipation of what more might be revealed by it.

"Show me more."

CHAPTER EIGHT

"The rain has stopped and it's dawn."
—James Corbin

I proceeded to work through the early hours with conflicting thoughts that made me doubt if all my effort would be worth it in the end. On more than one occasion, the idea of the sweet release of my handgun crossed my mind, but I could never find the courage to do it. Instead, I leaned back in my office chair, and relished tonight's discovery the best I could.

I spent a few more hours writing about the ancient world when the doorbell rang. I froze and furrowed my brow with confusion, and after a few moments, I stood and rushed to the door. Part of me guessed who would turn up at my house at 2 a.m., but the other part of me remained cautious with all the murders going on in the city.

"Who is it?" I asked through the door.

"You know who it is, Jay, open up, man," a familiar voice replied.

I smiled and opened the door to see my old college roommate, Joseph, standing on my front porch. Apparently, he had not bothered with an umbrella, as I watched him wipe the water from his face.

"You gonna let me in or what, man?" he asked as we shared our customary combination of a handshake and hug.

I gestured for him to step inside.

"Joe, man, what are you doing here at this time of night?" I asked.

Joseph locked the door behind him and turned back to me. "I came to check on you. We haven't talked in a couple of weeks."

"Man, it's 2 a.m. You never drop by this late," I observed. "Don't get me wrong, I'm not complaining. How is the American dream treating you?"

"Yeah, ha ha. No such thing for us," Joseph said with a sarcastic tone. "Man, everything is going great. The new position at work is going well, and the wife and kids are fine. You're right though, I didn't *just* drop by. Candace called me. She had some fucked-up things to say about you, and told me she had left. I think she called me to try to humiliate you more, and I have a feeling I'm not the only one she called. How are you holding up?"

"Figures. I don't think I'm her favorite person right now. Hey, man, let's go back to my office. I'm working on something I'd like to show you. We can talk some more there," I replied, shifting my shoulders uncomfortably and leading the way. The thought of rehashing the miserable events that had happened over the past several weeks wasn't ideal, and I didn't want to bring Joseph down since he had a newborn daughter to prioritize.

Once we reached my office, I slumped back into my leather chair and reluctantly relayed everything to him.

Joseph's eyes widened and his mouth dropped with disbelief and concern.

"James," Joseph pleaded, "you need to get some help. You must talk to someone— someone professional."

"Man, you know I can't do that. The minute someone finds out, I will have an entirely different set of problems on my hands. That's not what black men do. I can handle this myself."

"James, I'm a black man. Your depression isn't something for you to handle by yourself. Who gives a damn what others think? I get it. I know how we were raised. You deal with your problems alone and keep pressing forward, but that doesn't mean we were taught right. I need you to get professional help. I need my friend to get some help."

I sighed and turned my attention to the *Book of Blood* from Nadia's Voodoo shop. "Joe, I wanted to show you what I found. It could be what I need to help bring me out of this funk."

I grabbed the book and stared at Joseph with desperation. He eyed me with suspicion and raised an eyebrow, unconvinced that a mere book could cure my deep depression.

"I've found historical precedent to support everything I've been researching!" I explained, opening the book and turning the pages toward Joseph. "Remember the use of religion and the occult tools to manipulate the masses? The symbol of Ahura Mazda."

Joseph huffed at my disregard for his plea to get help. "Yes, I remember your theory."

"The Destructive Spirt. It wasn't Cyrus. It was Xerxes," I said with glee. "The Destructive Spirt was said to be the antithesis of Ahura Mazda and encompasses all that is the darker energy of the world. The entity is pure evil and thrives on providing the pathway to self-destruction and devastation of others by outside forces. It is the enemy of the lighted spirt, and the entity's name is Angra Mainyu, or Ahriman. That's what Xerxes used.

"Ahriman was Ahura Mazda's twin brother who fed off the most destructive aspect of men, destroying the soul of man and using that to feed his own power. The symbols on the cover of this book are similar, but this one represents the light of Ahura Mazda. The inverted triangle signifies the dark earth, and it encompasses the darkness of man's soul. The three points of the triangle denote three of the most destructive sins that can corrupt a man's soul — envy, greed, and wrath, and the red droplet underneath symbolizes the blood sacrificed to Ahriman to maintain his essence. Look for yourself."

"James, you're telling me that these gods are responsible for some of the most evil acts in Persian history? This is what Cyrus and Xerxes tapped into?" Joseph asked.

"No, men tapping into the essence of one of these gods is what's responsible for the evils of the Persian world," I corrected.

I looked back at the page and continued to read, excited to have someone's attention.

When I finished, I waited for Joseph to say something.

"It's unimaginable that such a desire for evil could be called upon by someone who had once been considered a good person. Doing it for power from someone already living in a morally gray area is understandable, but tapping into and harnessing a supernatural evil? You can't possibly get anyone to believe this without more evidence,

James. Besides, that book is written in gibberish. What is that, some sort of ancient language? How can you understand it?" Joseph said.

"We'll see, Joe," I replied, considering the valid point Joseph made. "But what do you mean, gibberish? This is written in perfect English."

I dipped my eyebrows with confusion and held the book open for Joseph to get a closer look again.

"James, I don't know what you're looking at, but that's not English. If it's about Persia like you said, then maybe it's Persian. It damn sure isn't English."

I scratched my head and squinted at the page, as I recalled Nadia's words to me that night. *The book found me*, I thought, but Joseph continued to speak.

"Look, man, I needed to check on you, but I have to get home before my wife starts to worry. I understand that diving into your work may help you escape, but you need to see someone, brother. I don't want to see you lock yourself away, possibly hurting yourself."

"I'll be okay, Joe," I assured him with a small smile. "I'm focused on teaching those kids and publishing my paper. Once things settle down, I'll be fine."

I didn't believe the words that flowed from my mouth, but I remained upbeat as I walked Joseph to the front door.

"I'll be over your way soon to see that beautiful little girl of yours," I said.

"See you soon, brother," Joseph replied, and he turned and ran to his car in the pouring rain.

I waved him off and headed back to my office, eager to return to the book. The stench of the stale pages had almost become therapeutic. The review of the incantation in the center of the book put a smile on my face.

It read: *The darkness will devour. Let the power of the destructive spirit consume. Blood is both the key and the door. Blood for essence.*

Some of the greatest leaders in Persian history are said to have harnessed this essence to gain power, such as Cambyses and Xerxes I, all in exchange for blood sourced from both the light and dark of humanity. Ahriman required blood of someone whose light had been extinguished by his essence, and the more damaged the soul, the more the essence could consume the body, and the more pain the destructive spirit could bring upon the earth.

I quivered with chills as I continued to read about the brutality inflicted on so many people in the pursuit of power or material riches in the name of Ahriman.

DESCENT OF A BROKEN MAN

I knew deep down that my theories were weak, and that no reputable publication would ever believe the mumbo jumbo of ghosts and gods, but with the documentation of the incantation, I could solidify the paper. Plus, the goal for the foreseeable future was to bring my new discovery to light and gain a little respect among my peers.

I threw my head back and wondered how on earth to prove my notions and show people hard evidence. Even I had to admit, everything I had read seemed a little far-fetched.

With a heavy sigh, I moved to the center of the room and searched for supplies I could use. There was only one way to establish my findings, and video evidence would be hard to dispute.

In the left corner of the office away from the desk, I spotted an old can of black paint under the windowsill. The sight of it brought back a stressful memory caused by the particular decorating taste of my wife.

"Who the hell wants black lawn furniture, anyway?" I scoffed, grabbing the paint.

I marched back to the center of my office and pulled the rug aside to expose the laminate floor underneath. I stirred the paint with the dried-out brush atop the lid and smeared the destructive spirit symbol on the floor.

Joe had a point—no reputable publication would take me seriously if I couldn't verify the practice. The sound of the storm intensified, and heavy raindrops pelted against the roof with rage.

I started on the interior of the triangle and beamed with excitement at the possibility of what could happen. Regardless of the air conditioning, sweat trickled down my forehead as I finished the final details of the destructive spirit symbol.

Once I stood to my feet, I stared at the drawing on the floor and grinned with self-satisfaction.

"Camera!" I shouted, moving to the opposite corner of the room, where the camera was placed atop a tripod.

I pointed the lens in the direction of the symbol and pressed record. I hurried to the desk and seized the *Book of Blood*, the heavy letter opener with a silver blade also gifted to me by my father, and kneeled inside the destructive spirit symbol on the floor.

My hands trembled as the thunder cracked open the sky; the sound reverberating through the windowpanes. I had never feared the sound of a thunderous storm before, but tonight was a different story.

I placed the book at the top of the inverted triangle and put my left hand on the wet circle inside. I raised the letter opener above my head and my heart raced with adrenaline.

"The darkness will devour. Let the power of the destructive spirit consume. Blood is both the key and the door. Blood for essence," I recited, and I drove the letter opener through the center of my hand and into the floor, pinning it firmly in place.

I roared with agonizing pain as blood poured from my hand and merged with the black paint. My face tensed and twisted with agony and my eyes bulged wider than ever before.

While groaning and wincing, I scanned the room for any signs of change, but nothing had happened. The storm continued to bellow through the atmosphere, and I had remained the same as before — alone and foolish.

I observed the damage done to my hand and my stomach knotted with unease, but I had to get the blade out of my flesh. I took a deep breath and wiggled it from side to side to ease it out of the wooden floor and out of my hand.

More blood flowed from the wound and I gripped my wrist in excruciating pain.

"You're a fucking idiot, James," I mumbled to myself, wincing and whimpering.

I snatched an old T-shirt hanging over the guest chair and wrapped it around my hand. My weak legs quivered as I stood again and staggered to the bottle of twelve-year-old scotch I kept on my bookshelf. I poured myself a tall glass to help calm my nerves and ease the pain.

"The rain has finally stopped, and dawn is setting in. I'm beginning my Saturday morning with a hole in my hand and a stiff drink. Man, you are such a winner, James," I mocked myself.

Just as I lifted my glass to take my first glug, my phone rang and intrusively filled the room. I flinched a little and slammed the glass back down.

"Hello!?" I yelled, my bloody hand soaking the T-shirt as it turned a crimson red.

On the other end of the line, a familiar voice spoke in a firm, haughty manner. "Hello, Mr. Corbin. This is Dr. Wilson. My apologies for such an early call on a Saturday. I need to see you in my office first thing Monday morning after homeroom. The matter is of significant importance."

I rolled my eyes at her voice and wondered why she couldn't call me at a reasonable time.

"Sure thing, Dr. Wilson, sure thing. I'll see you then," I replied, ending the call, and slamming the phone down.

DESCENT OF A BROKEN MAN

"There's always something with her, isn't there?" I huffed.

Even though I had no idea what this meeting with Dr. Wilson would be about, it didn't take a genius to figure out that a call from the principal on a Saturday morning was not good news. As the scotch kicked in, the aching soreness dulled, and the tension from the phone call dissipated.

Exhausted and no longer in the mood to finish my research, I slouched over my cluttered desk and scribbled my immediate findings of last night's ceremony, or lack thereof, onto a fresh piece of paper as I raised my wounded hand toward the ceiling.

Blood trickled down my palm as the new morning sun glared through the window and illuminated my desk. I stared at the bloody inscription on the ivory handle of the letter opener etched below its Christian cross, 'Your journey will be powerful. Love, Dad.' My faced winced again as the pain intensified.

"Yeah, Dad. I'm a real winner."

CHAPTER NINE

"I see that even a man of God, like yourself, is not without their own mistakes."—Detective Maor

---

Knock, knock, knock.

The door of the modest structure in the rear grounds of St. Mark's Catholic Church opened and a familiar pale face greeted Detective Maor.

"Hello. Can I help you, senora?" said the thin man with a smooth Italian accent.

His white, buttoned-down shirt and black slacks had been pressed with precision, so much so that not a wrinkle or crease could be seen. The tips of his square-toed shoes had been polished to make them shine like glass, and his hair was short and tapered.

"I'm Detective Maor with NOPD. Are you Deacon Bianchi?" she asked, suspecting a military background.

"Yes," he replied, his mannerisms rigid.

"Do you mind if we talk for a moment, sir?" Nola questioned, examining the details on the Deacon's face.

"Of course, Detective," Bianchi said with a coldness in his eyes that made Maor feel uneasy. "Please come in. Let's not let any more of the summer heat inside. This is the day the Lord has made. What can I help you with?" Bianchi tried to hide his icy glare with a grin, but it looked more like a grimace.

Maor entered the apartment in the rear of St. Mark's Church to see the sunlight piercing through the wide window nearest the door.

The residence smelled of pine oil and outdated furniture, but Maor ignored the smell and noted the small living room with mahogany floors and wooden shelving along the wall. The shelves were filled with old books on war, Christianity, philosophy, and history.

Maor suspected that the apartment, like the church itself, could have been built around fifty years ago. They never constructed roomy apartments back then, and there wasn't much living space in the apartment, even for one person.

"Please, make yourself comfortable, Detective. Would you like any tea?"

"Are you kidding? It's 95 degrees outside. I won't take up much of your time, Deacon. I just have a few questions," Maor replied, and remained in the middle of the room. "How are you enjoying your stay here in our great city, Deacon? I see you have made yourself at home in the community."

Maor studied Bianchi's eyes and mannerisms, expecting to catch him off guard with some easy questions and hoping to discover his social habits.

"I'm enjoying myself very much. The city has plenty of history and culture to offer, which has a special place in my heart, much like Italy. I see you have done some homework on me," Bianchi answered, his body language still and almost non-existent. "Although, the city is *covered* in sin and an overabundance of poor and troubled youth. This is a great place for a man of God to be. Lots of work to do."

"Mmm hmm. I see. What would that work involve exactly, Deacon?"

"Well, Detective, it involves doing moral work and making sure God gets the glory," he replied with a grin. "In particular, I like to work with young adults and set them on the correct path. Just as long as that path leads them to God. I like to think I'm saving their lives *and* souls in the process."

"I see. What happens if those young people refuse your help and won't take your God's path to improve their lives? What if they are defiant, Deacon?"

"God finds a way to reach all that can be saved, Detective. If they refuse, their sin will consume them."

Maor glared at Bianchi and tapped her foot with impatience. Listening to his self-righteous, religious babble made her stomach turn for she had heard it for years as a child.

Maor perused the room as Bianchi continued to blather about his God. She noticed his ceremonial robe hanging on a coat rack tucked away in the far corner. The sight of it brought back a flood of memories that caused sharp pains in her stomach, as if she had been whacked with something. The robe made her remember the disgust she had for organized religion and the painful memories that accompanied it.

"Reverend Jackson?" she interrupted.

Bianchi paused. "I beg your pardon?"

"Are you familiar with Reverend Jackson? He is the Reverend of Mt. Zion Baptist Church, here in the city."

"Why yes. Yes, I am. We recently worked together to launch our youth mentoring program, Serving Hope, Ambition, and Prayer, Every Day or S.H.A.P.E. Reverend Jackson and I shared the same objective of teaching young adults the hope and purpose God brings to one's life simply with faith and a little hard work. He was one of the first friends I made since planting roots here."

Bianchi ambled toward his bookshelf and admired the authors' impressive work. He grabbed one book in particular and held it with caution, like it was fragile. Bianchi read the title and smiled.

The Private Memoirs and Confessions of a Justified Sinner by James Hogg, Maor read from the spine of the book.

"Why do you ask, Detective?"

"He was murdered," Maor informed, probing him for a reaction.

Bianchi remained poised and displayed no reaction to the news about his supposed friend, but he glowered at Maor with viciousness in his eyes.

"That's unfortunate," Bianchi replied, still grinning.

He stood as still as a religious monument, and goosebumps raised on Maor's arms. Fear rushed through her body, and the heavy atmosphere in the small room made her feel trapped.

Maor edged closer to the window and peered out at the empty parking lot. She placed her right arm down by her waist side and rubbed her forearm against the butt of her .40 caliber Glock. An attempt to comfort herself.

"Forgive me if I don't seem surprised, Detective Maor," Bianchi said, breaking the tension in the room. "I'm in a bit of a state of shock, you see. We were just together at the Center about a week ago talking about the best way to get through to a troublesome kid we came across. We disagreed about it, though. I wanted a more traditional method of incorporating the Lord into the young man's life, but the Reverend wanted to mix the Lord's teaching with a new age approach, which involved positive thinking. It sounded quite hokey to me, to be honest," Bianchi explained, looking away from the Detective. "When was he murdered? Do you have any leads, Detective?"

"Two days ago. I'm afraid that's all I'm able to divulge, Deacon. Do you know of anyone who wanted to hurt Reverend Jackson? Why would a man of God have someone after him?"

Maor knew there had been a religious motive behind the murder, but she was more interested in Bianchi's response.

"I don't have the foggiest idea, Detective. The Reverend was a well-respected man, and it pains me that someone took him from this Earth. However, given the path he was on, maybe it was God's will."

"Excuse me? What would make you say that?" Maor asked.

"Well, you see, Detective, as leaders of the church, we should not give any credibility to such things as astrology, tarot card readings, and other superstitious nonsense. It's idolatry and against God!" Bianchi barked, gripping his book so hard the tips of his fingers turned white.

He placed the book down and unbuttoned the cuffs of his shirt on both arms. Bianchi rolled up his sleeves in the neatest manner possible and exposed a small tattoo of a torch that looked as if it were done in prison.

No military man would have that poor of ink, Maor thought.

"I see even a man of God, like yourself, are not without their own mistakes," Maor said, nodding toward his tattoo.

"Oh, this," Bianchi acknowledged. "A regret from a misspent youth, Detective. I did it as a reminder of my burning optimism in man. A little shortsighted, I know."

"I see," Maor said. "Well, thank you for your time, Deacon. Good luck with your endeavors here in the city. I will be in contact with you if I have any more questions."

Maor hurried to the door, unwilling to wait for a reply from the Deacon, and yanked it open.

The humid air hit her face, but the thick mugginess was better than the tension in Bianchi's apartment.

"See you soon, Detective," Bianchi shouted after her, meeting her gaze with a cold smile.

Maor shut the door behind her and left Deacon Bianchi in the middle of his living room. She rushed back to her car and recollected the disturbing images from her childhood. Just as one particular memory made her stomach twist with discomfort, she halted a couple of yards away from her car. She looked back at the closed door of Deacon Bianchi's apartment.

"He *was* one of the first friends I made..." she mumbled under her breath, repeating Bianchi's words. "*Was?* That's the past tense. You knew. A misspent youth, huh? Bullshit, Deacon. What are you hiding?"

Maor scrambled into her car, eager to get as far away from St. Mark's Church as possible. Her uneasiness was not only a result of Deacon Bianchi's creepy demeanor, but also the sight of his ceremonial robe. The memories of being raised as a Catholic girl in a city with a large presence of Catholicism were hard enough, but the terrifying things she had witnessed had pushed her away from the church and from God himself.

When Maor turned fourteen, Father Williams chose her to be his personal assistant, a responsibility that filled her with joy, even if she would just be writing letters and answering the phone. Father Williams had known Maor all her life and had watched her grow into a responsible teenager, so she knew she could trust him with her life.

But when Maor made her way to the office section of the church, fitted with plush red carpet and well-insulated walls, the door had been left slightly ajar, and she heard faint whimpering as she approached.

"There is no need to cry," a familiar voice spoke.

Maor inched closer to the door and peered through the gap of the office door. She spotted Father Williams in the center of the room with his back facing the door, speaking to someone inside.

"Your time is up, harlot. God has spoken. You walk around this city exposing your flesh like a whore; you are sin!" Father Williams spat.

Young Maor noticed red stains on the right side of Father Williams' robe and a large hunting knife with a black handle in his hand. Streaks of blood covered the sharp blade, and Maor's eyes widened. She slowly pushed the door open, and she froze at the sight before her.

Father Williams stood in front of a teenage girl whose hands and feet were bound. Clear packaging tape covered her mouth and deep cuts burned into her bare limbs. The girl writhed in the wooden chair and moaned for help as she met Maor's eyes. Father Williams turned and saw Maor in the doorway.

Maor screamed and ran out of the church. Father Williams chased her, begging her to stop, but he could not catch her.

Maor never looked back, even as an adult.

Maor snapped out of her horrific flashback as she parked her car outside the police station.

"Thankful they caught and arrested the murderous son of a bitch," she hissed at the thought of Father Williams.

From that day forward, Maor's trust in the church shattered.

"Never again," she muttered, scowling at her naive past as she headed back into the safety of the station.

CHAPTER TEN

"Yes!"
—James

After a long, disappointing weekend, I stepped outside on Monday morning and glanced up at a bright blue sky. The warm sun and the birds' melody welcomed me as I yawned with exhaustion, and the smell of recently cut grass completed the scene.

Despite the fine summer weather, I sighed as I trudged toward my car and dreaded the day ahead. I wanted to stay in bed all day but calling in sick when Wilson awaited my arrival in her office wouldn't help my already tenuous relationship with her. Plus, I needed the money.

I slipped into my car and slid the keys into the ignition, but when I gripped the gear stick and steering wheel, I winced with pain.

I didn't know what could be worse, the agony I had caused myself the previous night, or my coworkers and students questioning what had happened to my hand.

In the distance, the school bell sounded through my car windows and a knot tightened in my stomach.

I had managed to be late... again.

I grabbed my bag from the back seat and sprinted toward the school entrance; my hurrying beat me into a sweat and caused my shirt to untuck itself. I reached for the door handle with my left hand and forgot all about the gash through my palm. A flash of ferocious pain rushed through my entire body and caused me to bellow in agony. A few late students stared at me and the fresh blood soaked the white bandage, but I couldn't stop or take a trip to the nurse; I had to get to class. As I adjusted the briefcase in my hand and turned a sharp corner, Dr. Wilson stood in the center of the corridor with her head tilted down. Her rectangular glasses were perched on the tip of her nose and her thin lips were tense.

She raised a displeased eyebrow at me and beckoned me over with one curled finger.

"Here we go," I mumbled under my breath with a huff of frustration. Dr. Wilson turned on her heel and led me up the hallway.

As we passed the stairs that led to the second floor, a tight ball of paper struck the side of my head. A group of students guffawed at the accurate hit, and I turned to see Damon and Cynthia among the group, a popular couple in the school.

"Heads up, Mr. C!" Damon said, smirking as he passed me.

I glowered at him for attempting to humiliate me and continued to follow Dr. Wilson to her office, shutting the door behind me when we arrived.

The repugnant stench of foot odor and cheap perfume assaulted my nose and stomach yet again, and Dr. Wilson resumed her seat in her leather chair. I sat across from her for the hundredth time and waited for her to speak. Dr. Wilson clasped her hands together, interlocking her fingers, and eyed me like a hawk.

"Mr. Corbin, I see you have an injury on your hand. It seems to be pretty fresh as you are still bleeding profusely. Since you just arrived here on campus, I would assume this is not a work-related injury?" she coldly asked.

"No, I sliced it repairing the blade on my lawn mower. It's no big deal."

"Good. I would hate to have to fill out any injury reports on your behalf. Now, for the reason I wanted this conference, did you address the subject of religion, specifically Christianity, in your class two weeks ago?" Mrs. Wilson asked.

I furrowed my brow with confusion. "Yes, I did. You know I did... we have already discussed it. The lecture regarded the similarities between the origins and foundations of several religions, from a historic point of view, of course. I intended to stimulate dialogue in the class as they all appeared disinterested before."

DESCENT OF A BROKEN MAN

My heart throbbed after defending my position, and my breathing became short and shallow. Sweat formed on my forehead and my hands trembled with the anticipation of Dr. Wilson's response.

"Religion is not a topic for discussion within these walls, Mr. Corbin! You know the rules. Now, because of you, I have angry parents and students who feel that you have belittled their beliefs. Some are threatening litigation, and now, the school board is involved. Do you understand the position you have put this school in?" Mrs. Wilson lectured.

My shoulders tensed and my skin became clammy, making me sweat even more.

Before I could respond, Dr. Wilson successfully put the final nail in my already troubled life. "As of now, you are suspended without pay effective immediately. If I were you, Mr. Corbin, I wouldn't expect to return to this school at all."

"Wait, what? Why? You must be kidding me!" I exclaimed. "Please don't do this. Please!"

"My God, look at how pathetic you are. Pack your shit and leave the facility, Mr. Corbin."

I gripped Dr. Wilson's desk with both hands and my fingertips turned pale as rage fired through me. The pain from the stab wound on my hand was intense as blood trickled from my hand on to her desk.

"Who are you calling pathetic, little woman?" I asked. Every muscle in my body was tightening as if they were being ripped off the bone. "I have worked—"

Dr. Wilson frowned. "Who the hell do you—"

"DON'T YOU DARE INTERRUPT ME!" I roared, slamming both fists onto Dr. Wilson's desk. My voice dropped two octaves deeper than normal and distorted. After I slammed my fist, a small wave of energy reverberated from the desk and traveled across the room blowing paper onto the floor and pushed Dr. Wilson back into her chair.

"What is that? Is that fear on your face, Wilson?"

"I—I don't know what just happened. "P—please leave," she stuttered. Panic covered Dr. Wilson's face and her lips quivered.

I leaned back in the chair in shame and took a moment before I stood. "This is not the last you'll hear from me, Wilson. I promise you that," I said, as I slammed the door behind me and left the campus.

Later that evening, I continued to sit in the brown armchair that looked out into the neighborhood and reflect on my day.

"What was happening to me in Dr. Wilson's office?" I mumbled in frustration.

The stillness of the room made me realize how empty the house had become without Candace, but the orange sunset provided a little comfort as I wallowed in regret and anger.

The immense effort and long hours I had put into my position had all been for nothing. All those years of people degrading me, doubting me, taking advantage of me, and lying to me—all to be fired at the end of it for *doing my job*.

As my mind flooded with the emotional trauma of getting fired, injuring my hand, and Candace leaving, my breathing intensified and the pressure in my head made my eyes throb in their sockets. I gasped for air as much as I could, but the muscles in my throat swelled, closing my airways. My hands shook with rage and my mind began to quiet.

As tears fell from my eyes, I grabbed my 9mm caliber handgun from the table beside me and pressed the end of the barrel against my temple. The cool metal soothed me, like a cold compress on a migraine.

I had always heard that moments before death, one's life flashes before their eyes. Their victories, defeats, family, and childhood memories, but not for me. From the moment I decided to do this, I had felt nothing but rage.

As my index finger tensed and slowly squeezed the trigger, my mind remained as quiet as the room around me. The only other sound was the subtle squeak of the trigger as my finger wavered in my hesitation.

"James!" a menacing voice called out.

At first, I didn't know if the voice spoke in my head because of my current state, or if there was someone else in the house.

Fighting the uncontrollable agony in my head, I struggled to my feet and scanned the room.

"Who's there?" I yelled, half expecting a troublesome student to jump out, but no one responded.

I crept through the different rooms of the house to find the owner of the ominous voice, but I found no one.

"You should know, boy, for you summoned me," the voice

rumbled in my mind. "It's been hard for you, hasn't it, James? The world can't see you and the sadness is overwhelming, consuming, especially with so much failure in every aspect of your miserable life. The world is cruel enough to black men without the weight of depression looming over you."

My eyes widened with a mixture of fear and flabbergast. "How—"

"I need to thank you for awakening me," the voice continued.

"Ahriman?"

"Yes!" the voice growled with pride. "I felt your sacrifice. I felt your pain, James, and it was enough. I know what your heart desires and I will help you get it. You are who you think you are."

The barrage of words from Ahriman reverberated in my head.

"Say yes and you will get your respect. You will get what you've earned. I will take the sadness away and give you my essence. I only ask for blood in return," Ahriman said, his voice pushing the physical limits of my mind.

Ahriman's silence after his offer provided little relief. My troubled past and failures flooded my memories. Death would have been a welcoming peace for me, but Ahriman's offer and the chance to prove others wrong and make them suffer for it tapped into something inside me.

"Yes!" I yelled, my voice cracking. "I will give you blood. Just make it stop. I'll do anything to make it all stop."

Sinister laughter filled the room and a wave of forceful energy pushed out in all directions, knocking me to the floor. A moment of peace set in for the first time in years. No emotional pain, no physical pain, no one belittling me and no depression.

The last remnants of sunlight flickered away as the sun descended behind the horizon, but my skin seared with heat as if the ball of fire focused only on me.

I bellowed in scorching agony as the veins in my forehead bulged and the pounding pressure in my head burst the vessels in my eyes. Tears of blood poured from my sockets and singed my cheeks on the way down, and my fingers grew inches longer, with sharp claws bursting from the tips. The bones in my face shattered, cracking like wood in a roaring fire, but they reformed into a skull the size of a mythological beast's. Leather-like skin covered my new beastly bones, and triangular teeth protruded from my mouth, extending over my lips.

The inverted triangle of Ahriman charred into my chest, and once again, silence fell upon the room.

As exhaustion overshadowed the burning pain, the room darkened. I felt different, stronger. Yet there was another presence inside me, infecting me. It pushed me to kill and gave me the perfect beastly form to do it as my consciousness slipped into the background.

I stood in the middle of the living room, a large beastly figure, and panted with thirst. My eyes glowed yellow as I stared in the mounted mirror.

Needing to quench its desires, I planted my monstrous foot into the floor and powered through the front door, smashing it to pieces and charging into the street. My powerful animal like legs allowed me to leap from the middle of the urban street onto a neighboring rooftop and jumped over the houses toward the Treme neighborhood, specifically the world-famous Armstrong Park.

CHAPTER
ELEVEN

"Anyone could have been in this park tonight."
—Detective Maor

Detective Maor surveyed the scene in Armstrong Park as rows of oak trees bordered the grounds.

As dawn approached, Maor still couldn't get past her perplexity at the carnage in the double homicide. She had seen dozens of slain bodies this year alone, often young black men involved in drug and gang violence, but she couldn't work out the motive behind these victims, and the sight made her uneasy.

The gore didn't bother her; Maor's discomfort came from the rage and physicality behind the attacks.

As Detective Maor analyzed the wounds on the lifeless young couple, she stretched the muscles in her neck at the sight of the young woman's hard, dry lips and pale skin. Her eyes looked as though they had frosted over, and her stiff hand extended out in front of her, a last second reach for her male companion. The peridot promise ring on her finger and the short distance between them implied to Maor that they were a couple.

If the young lady didn't deeply care for the man, he could have convinced her to run, and she would have been much farther away or would have gotten away altogether, she thought.

The young man beside her had an athletic physique, which made Maor wonder how big or strong the perpetrator was.

Maor crouched next to the pool of blood between the bodies

and peered into the young man's wide eyes. She noticed a hole the size of a softball in his chest, and glanced back at the young lady; a gaping cut across her throat.

"This is vicious," she whispered to herself as she stood to her feet.

"Detective!" a young officer yelled, grabbing Maor's attention as he approached. "No weapons have been left behind, and we haven't found any witnesses. The young man had movie ticket stubs in his pocket from last night, and both also had school IDs. He lives a few blocks from here. According to their school IDs from Robert E. Lee High School, their names are Damon Fuller and Cynthia Henderson. They must have cut through the park to get to this place. I know I'm new, but I've never seen anything like this, except in the movies. The city is kinda living up to its reputation as the murder capital of the nation, huh?"

"Thank you, Officer. Log the IDs, ticket stubs, and wallet contents into Central Evidence. Let's get the coroner out here," Maor interrupted, perturbed at his lack of professionalism. "Hey, Bryant! I need you and your rookie to get the hell off my crime scene. I don't know what you are teaching him and why he touched the bodies, but you know better. Make sure your initial report reflects it as well," she lectured.

Maor grabbed her notepad from her back pocket and scribbled her observations, scowling at the officer's actions.

Detective Maor knew a scene like this would garner a lot of attention, so touching the bodies before the coroner arrived would be a big violation for her, and she couldn't have any holes when it went to court.

Maor stepped away from the bodies and searched for anything that could give insight into the night's events, but all she saw were empty crack vials, used needles, and broken glass scattered along the stained concrete near the young couple.

"Anyone could have been in this park tonight," she said to herself.

The walkway of the crime scene sat in the sun-lit shadow of the Municipal Auditorium, a 1930s structure that had stood the test of time and had become a staple of the Treme neighborhood. However, these dark times put people off using it, so the abandoned building now had its fair share of graffiti tags and vagrants who often used the space as their personal entertainment center.

Detective Maor stared at the structure from a short distance, admiring its durability and elegant arched entrances made from stone.

For the first time that week, she smiled at the beauty before her, until she noticed movement under one of the archways. Detective Maor squinted and crept closer to the figure, her heart rate increasing.

The silhouette shuffled on the ground, attempting to gain cover behind one of the stone arches, and Maor edged toward it.

Upon closer inspection, she noticed the figure to be a homely-dressed old man in what could have been a white shirt and grey pants, but the accumulation of dirt from months of sleeping on the filthy streets had turned the shirt gray.

The old man sat with his back against the wall and his eyes wide open. His unkept face made his facial expression hard to identify, but Maor recognized the look in his eyes.

"Sir!" she yelled, kneeling next to him. "Sir, can you hear me?! Are you okay? How long have you been here?"

"I've — I've been here all night. I have the right to be here, cop. I know what you want. What did I see, r-right? Is — is that what you want to know?" the man stammered. "It came out of the trees."

"It?" Maor questioned, a crease forming between her eyebrows.

"It was huge! The damn thing lurked in the trees above those kids and watched, like it was hunting. It was unnatural. Beastly, like the Philistine giant, Goliath. Only this time, David got his ass whipped! That thing wasn't human!" the man cried, his lip quivering as he bawled.

The old man sat up in frustration, eager to change the subject and end the conversation with the detective. "I bet a nice stiff bottle of Night Train would hit the spot right now."

The stench of stale alcohol filled the nearby area that surrounded the vagrant. Maor's nostrils had gotten used to this smell over the years, but it still lingered in the pit of her stomach sometimes.

Of course, she thought. *This is New Orleans. Tales of voodoo, vampires, and werewolves galore. There is always some superstitious foolishness used to explain something they don't understand in this city.*

"What's your name, sir?" Detective Maor inquired.

"Jack."

"Give me something I can work with, Jack, and I'll put you in a nice motel room, so you can shower and eat the fattest po-boy I can find, along with a six-pack of beer," Detective Maor coaxed, trying to entice a realistic story from the witness. "Whoever murdered those kids is very dangerous. You have to give me something better than monsters falling from trees."

"Lady, I know what I saw, and I'm telling you, that thing was not human. Its face was animal like. Almost like a cougar or lion or something. After it killed those kids, it laughed and took off deeper into the Treme like a damn jungle cat. I could lie to you and take you up on your offer, but I've seen nothing like that before in my life. If you don't believe me, then leave me the hell alone. I have some drinking to do."

Detective Maor was taken aback by Jack's assertiveness, but she still didn't believe his tall tale. She stood to her feet and ambled away, disappointed that she had wasted time with a drunken witness, only to see a cluster of beat reporters a dozen feet away, jotting down whatever they overheard.

"How the hell did they get in here?" she yelled at a couple of uniformed officers nearby, pointing at the reporters. "For fuck's sake! Can we get this area taped off, please?"

As Detective Maor made her way back to the bodies, she noticed the coroner's van arrived and hurried over to the scene. They placed Damon and Cynthia into body bags and loaded them into the van, leaving their blood to be slowly absorbed by the concrete.

Detective Maor hoped that a thorough look into the victims' lives would shed a light on any potential leads, because whomever had killed them was capable of a brutality many do not possess.

The crackle of Maor's handheld police radio interrupted her thoughts, only to inform everyone of another shooting in her district.

There's a surprise, Maor thought with sarcasm, and she stood in the middle of the pavement with a heavy sigh.

In a city so full of art and love, people were dying.

"Let's get hold of those kids' parents," Maor said to one of the last remaining uniformed officers on the scene. "Ugh, I hate doing notifications. There is no good way to break the news to a parent that their child was killed. Officer, contact the desk officer and have them find out the name and number of the principal at Lee High School. I need to talk to everyone."

CHAPTER TWELVE

"Those scratches look like some sort of animal put them there."
—Officer Greyson

"New Orleans Police Department! Sir! Are you okay? Sir, police!" a voice echoed out. "Sir, are you okay? We're coming in!"

I peeled my eyes open and blinked erratically, adjusting to the bright sunlight blaring into the room.

"H-hello?" I croaked, my throat dry and hoarse.

I raised my head to scan my surroundings, and my blurry vision soon focused on the familiar furniture in my living room. The wool fabric of the couch brushed against my bare back as I sat up, and the soles of my feet enjoyed the warmth of the wooden floor. My head, on the other hand, throbbed as if I had a bad hangover, and sweat trickled down my face.

When I looked up, the uniformed police officers who stood in the open doorway came into focus.

"Yes, Officers. Is there something wrong?" I asked.

"We should be asking you that, Mr. Corbin," an officer replied.

I dipped my brow. "How do you know my name?"

"Your neighbor. He saw your front door split into pieces and figured someone had broken in. You mind telling us what happened here?" the officers inquired, each scanning the area. "How did your door get like this? Your neighbor said he heard a thunderous boom last night and saw a large man in the middle of the street. Were you home last night?"

"No, I had a rough day yesterday. Got fired from my job, so I didn't want to be home alone. I took a bottle of vodka and walked the streets. So, my neighbor heard all of that last night and waited until the morning to call? What an asshole. He always was though."

My recollection of last night remained foggy in my mind. Flashes of random images flooded my head, but I couldn't make sense of them.

The officers shared glances, likely passing judgment on my behavior, but as they continued to look around, one of them spotted my 9mm handgun on the floor.

"Gun!" one of them shouted.

The other officer placed his hand on his holstered weapon and directed his attention toward me.

"That's mine!" I blurted. "I told you; I got low yesterday. I thought about checking out, but— I changed my mind," I said, shifting my shoulders uncomfortably.

One officer picked up the gun, ejected the magazine, and released the round from the chamber. "Mr. Corbin, I'm going to go ahead and run this in the system. I'll be in the car, partner, if you need me."

The remaining officer nodded and turned back to me.

"Mr. Corbin," he said. "I'm not sure I understand what you're telling me..."

The officer continued to question me, but the previous night's events diverted my attention. Images of blood and terror from every strike repeated in my head, and unknowingly brought a slight grin to my face, but the officer raised his voice and reminded me of his presence.

"Obviously, this was not a robbery, Mr. Corbin. So, how about you be straight with me?" He walked a little further into the room, squaring his shoulders in my direction, but I had grown tired of his tone already.

"How about you get the fuck out of my house! I didn't call you. There's no victim, so there's no crime. Give me my gun and get the hell out of my house!" I yelled.

Eager for confrontation, I got to my feet, still shirtless, and relished in the opportunity to show the officer that I would not tolerate the disrespectful tone.

"We'll leave when we are done with our investigation. How about you take a seat before you do or say something you will regret? I get it. You got fired and had a bad day. Had a few drinks even. That doesn't explain the door, Mr. Corbin. Easy question, what happened to the door?"

"It's my fucking door. If I want to break it to pieces 'cause I'm pissed off, I can do that," I answered, as I stared him down.

"Mr. Corbin, we will document our encounter for today and forward the report to our burglary detective for possible follow up. If you notice anything missing, please contact us. Oh, and if you are in any way responsible for any crimes committed last night, I'll be in touch."

The officer glared at me as his partner reentered the room.

"It's clean," he interrupted, setting my gun on the chair. "Is there a problem in here, partner?"

"No, there is no problem. Just finishing up my interview," the officer said, keeping his eyes on me. "One other question. Do you have a dog or some kind of pet, Mr. Corbin?"

"No. No pets. Why is that important?"

The officer nodded and pointed at the damaged floor. "Those scratches look like some sort of animal put them there."

My heart pounded as memories of my transformation reentered my mind.

"Oh, no, I did it moving furniture," I lied.

As both officers finally left me in peace, I resumed my seat on the couch and filtered through the events I could remember.

Something happened the night before. I couldn't quite put my finger on *what* occurred or all the details, but I had the feeling it was the start of something big.

CHAPTER THIRTEEN

"No doubt why this city is damned."
—Deacon Bianchi

As Deacon Bianchi traveled through the Lower Ninth Ward with the windows of his car rolled down, he took in the surroundings of the busy neighborhood. An area filled with energetic bounce music and social gatherings with lots of food for a weekday.

Bianchi enjoyed driving his white Cadillac around the city; its new model garnered him some positive attention, and it proved to be a great conversation starter when he approached potentially dangerous youth. His car also allowed him to listen to Bach, Beethoven, and Chopin with little effort when he cruised around the city. The harmony of his favorite classical tracks calmed him, which added to the notion that classical music was the only acceptable type in God's eyes. Its beauty rivaled only by the word itself.

"The Lucifer-invoking nature of *their* music is revolting; no doubt why this city is damned," he proclaimed.

As Bianchi rolled from block to block, the young people of the neighborhoods engaged in pickup basketball games. He beamed at their ingenuity of using milk crates nailed to telephone poles as makeshift basketball hoops, and he enjoyed the innocent scene of kids tossing footballs in the middle of the streets and jumping rope to occupy their time. He admired them for finding happiness among the violence, drugs, and murder.

As Bianchi traveled farther into the Lower Ninth Ward, his luxury vehicle attracted the attention of three high-school-aged men on the corner who watched him as he drove by. Their baggy clothes and shiny gold teeth were a shared trait among them; only two out of a million reasons why Bianchi became convinced there was no need to salvage their lost souls.

Bianchi rolled up his car window and lifted his nose in the air.

Although his sole purpose for being in the area was to find more troubled youth for S.H.A.P.E., Bianchi did not bother to convey the word of God to most older teenagers. He preferred to reach them at a younger age when they could still be influenced by the word.

Bianchi drove deeper into the neighborhood, but the poorer the area became, the more judgmental glares he received.

Feeling tired of driving, Bianchi pulled over near the corner of Jourdan Ave. and North Villere St., which faced the Industrial Canal, a throughway for ships and barges traveling to and from the Mississippi River.

The neighborhood that surrounded him seemed peaceful compared to the others he had driven through, and the families also had more material possessions in comparison. The pleasant sound of children's laughter echoed through the hot air as two kids scribbled with chalk on the ground, and Bianchi smiled to himself.

"God has truly touched this block," he said with pride.

As Bianchi watched the kids, the last shotgun house on the corner caught his attention. It had an unusual sign staked into the front lawn, so his curiosity propelled him to drive over for a closer look.

The old home with a red and black theme looked abandoned. The old black paint peeled off the exterior; the window shutters were partially detached, as they hung below the windows and no longer served any real purpose. The front lawn was unkept and grew long enough to start its engulfment of the stairs, which led to the front porch. Bianchi pulled up anyway and read the handmade sign: 'Priestess Nadia's Voodoo Emporium.'

Bianchi's jaw tensed at the words and he scowled in disgust. He left his car and stood before the house.

"Sacrilege," he spat. "Let's see who's home, shall we?"

Bianchi approached the ebony-colored door and banged on the wood. As he waited for a response, the faint smell of burnt flowers crept from behind the door and filled him with nausea.

"It's open," a faint feminine voice yelled.

Bianchi furrowed his brow and edged his way into the house; the stench was even more unbearable.

Old books, crystals, trinkets, and religious paraphernalia filled the cramped living room, transforming it into a makeshift storefront. Four wooden bookshelves that reached the low ceiling sat in the middle of the floor with a few square tables surrounding them.

"How can I help you today?" Priestess Nadia asked from across the room.

Nadia sat on a wooden stool near the windows that looked out onto the quiet neighborhood, and one of the square tables stood beside her, a receipt booklet, a journal, and an old cash box on top.

Upon closer inspection, Bianchi noticed that the books were in alphabetical order, and the trinkets and statues were all perfectly centered and facing front.

"Please tell me, what is this place?" Bianchi asked with a fake but pleasant smile. "I was in the neighborhood and came across your sign staked in the front yard."

"Well, your accent clearly tells me you're not from 'round here. But I know who you are. You are getting a reputation in this city, Deacon. Your good works, along with your colleagues at S.H.A.P.E., have been praised by some of the elder people here in the neighborhood," Nadia said with a smile on her face.

"Well, thank —"

"I said *some*," Nadia interrupted, her smile reverting to an inquisitive frown.

She stood from her stool and her old joints clicked and creaked like she hadn't moved for days.

Bianchi eyed her with caution as she reached for her cherry-red cane that had two handcrafted snake heads at the top. The menacing craftmanship of the cane didn't match the pleasant aesthetics of Nadia's gray curls and warm brown eyes, but it seemed to serve as a warning.

"It appears you have me at a disadvantage, Signora. Of course, I am Deacon Bianchi of St. Mark's Catholic Church, and you are?" he eagerly asked.

"I am Priestess Nadia. At least that's what most folks call me 'round here. Although I've been given many names in my time."

Nadia hobbled toward Bianchi like a fragile grandmother, and her cane tapped rhythmically as it struck the hardwood floor.

Bianchi continued. "So, what is this place? What are you selling here?"

"Selling? I'm not selling anything. There are things for sale here, but when you come here, you have already been sold," Nadia stated, remaining cryptic.

"I've been sold? This is obviously a voodoo shop, and your trinkets are false gods," Bianchi barked, a tone of superiority slipping through. His eyes wandered to a Falcata sword mounted on a shelf nearby.

"Oh. I see. And what, pray tell, do you think I do here exactly? I'm asking because you seem to have it all figured out," Nadia challenged, but Bianchi said nothing, so the Priestess scoffed and continued. "I'm here to help others find their paths through my religion, so they can go on their own spiritual journey. Unlike you, most people who walk in here are either searching for direction or are tourists looking for an experience. Whatever the reason someone wanders in here, their energy is evident to me. These things find those who should acquire them, and the items will guide them in return."

Bianchi's traditionalist ideology did not allow for a woman to speak to him in that manner. However, his ability to maintain his calm composure was more important to him than his establishment of control.

"With all due respect, Signora, the only thing you guide your patrons toward is the road to hell. Your religion is false. Your God is false. Simply put, the idea of your beliefs is such childish superstition. The very presence of your so-called *emporium* is an affront to God," he replied; again, his eyes wandered toward the sword.

"Superstitions?" Nadia asked, keeping her cool. "Do you not feel the energy in this room, Deacon? Or is your religion blinding you? The energy in this room is ever present. It shows up in color. It surrounds the items in the room and the people who enter. For instance, your energy and its dark purple haze matches this compact sword you've been eyeing up a couple times since you've been here."

Bianchi shifted with unease and glanced away from the sword.

"You're mistaken. I have only eyed things with disgust since my arrival," he defended, trying to fathom how on earth Nadia knew.

"It's interesting that you're drawn to it," Nadia continued, ignoring Bianchi's resistance. "This sword has a bloody history, and once belonged to one of the most misguided, evil Voodoo priests in times gone by. He forged it in tribute to Hannibal, a manifestation of his Falcata. The blade is not only sharp but is said to have... additional qualities. Yet, it seems to be drawn to you and you to it; a man of the cloth. Is there something you're hiding, Deacon?"

Nadia's eyes locked onto Bianchi's face, and he stared at the sword and its unique appearance.

The sword's handle had been crafted from bone with several ridges carved on both sides and a skull at the base. The obsidian blade reflected the smallest measure of light, and it appeared to be single-edged near the hilt and double-edged near the point. Perfect for close combat.

A sense of forbidden excitement coursed through Bianchi as if he appreciated the beauty of a nearby woman, but despite his desire for its power, he maintained his calm demeanor and moved his eyes back to Priestess Nadia, giving her a stale, emotionless grin.

"I am in the business of saving souls, and that can only be done through the one true God, through the purity of Catholicism and Christianity," Bianchi answered.

The Priestess smiled at Bianchi; her straight teeth the color of his robes contrasting with her dark complexion and piercing brown eyes.

"I see. Catholicism and Christianity? Apparently, your arrogance is only surpassed by your ignorance, Deacon Bianchi. I'm not going to get into the intricacies of my religion, but much like you coming in here and telling me what should be, it was slave traders and slave owners who tried to outlaw African religions. Forcing Roman Catholicism upon the slaves only pushed them to intertwine aspects of traditional Voudon, which birthed what you know as Voodoo."

Bianchi opened his mouth to interrupt Nadia, but he couldn't get a word in edgeways.

"You see, Deacon, your presence here, along with this conversation is a repeat of history, and not without its irony. A white man coming to *my* land to tell me what's good for me *and* to push his religion upon me!"

Nadia turned away from Bianchi and plodded back to her seat near her window, her cane tapping the wood once again.

"This place is for those who are looking for guidance or those who are looking for knowledge. You don't fit any of those, Deacon. Please, see yourself out."

Deacon Bianchi glared at her with contempt in his eyes. "Well, Madam, Hell awaits you. I hope to finish this discussion another time. Arrivederci."

He sauntered out of the makeshift store and left the door agape as one last act of disrespect to her sanctuary, as the priestess scribbled into the notebook on the table.

"You won't have to wait long for Hell to be at your doorstep," he mumbled in his descent down the stairs.

CHAPTER
FOURTEEN

"Are you telling me this isn't a gimmick, and that this psycho actually believes in what he is doing?"—Detective Maor

A few days after the events that took place in Armstrong Park, my own D-Day, I nabbed a charming little spot by the window in my favorite uptown coffee shop, The Redd Bean, and stuck my head into a newspaper.

"Hey, Mrs. Redd. Let me get a coffee. Black," I said with a warm smile, as I rubbed the palms of my hands together in anticipation.

"James! How are you, young man?" Mrs. Redd asked as she leaned on the service counter, patting my clasped hands, accompanied by a small leap that helped her plant a quick kiss upon my cheek. "Henry, bring James a black coffee. I never knew you liked it black. I've noticed you switched for a few days now. You always have a coffee with milk and chicory."

"Thanks, Mrs. Redd, and yeah, fancied a change today. How's your morning going so far?"

"Child, we are fine. I have to say, I'm sorry about your job, but I'm happy to see you in here every morning," Mrs. Redd sympathized. "On top of it all, our granddaughter agreed to work with us part-time while in school. We are ecstatic!"

"Donna will work here? How has she been?" I asked.

"Baby, she is great. Got into pharmacy school over at Xavier. She'll be happy to see you."

"I haven't seen her in quite a while. I knew she was a smart one.

Thanks again, Mrs. Redd." I sipped my coffee, and the robust flavor was satisfying as it made its way to my stomach. I turned and provided a thumbs up to Mr. Redd in appreciation as I sat at a nearby table and stared out the window.

The hustle of the early morning rush put my stomach on edge as I thought about my former commute. I should feel disheartened about the loss of my teaching job, but the sentiment was not there, especially since I had the house to myself, and without the troubles between myself and my wife. As a matter of fact, I had experienced fewer mood swings and symptoms of depression and anxiety since Candace's departure and the essence.

I leaned back in the chair as if a huge weight was lifted off my shoulders. I turned the page in my newspaper and read the bold headline at the top.

'New Orleans Murder Rate Highest in Nation. Another Execution-Style Murder. Police Continue to Deny Serial Killer. Four More Mutilated Bodies Found in Uptown, Goliath Killer Suspected.'

"Goliath? There's that name again," I whispered. "It doesn't matter. All that matters is the blood, and there will be more. Ahriman took away my pain and I must hold up my end. I never thought I could do the things I've done, but if it will make my life better as a result — I'll keep doing it."

The bell above the door chimed and a woman entered the coffee shop. She closed the door behind her and scanned the room; her brow tensed.

Her caramel skin and shoulder length hair glistened even in the harsh fluorescent light, and her blue-collared blouse and fitted black pants enhanced her curvy figure.

When she focused her hazel eyes in my direction, she marched toward me.

I raised my brow with surprise and smiled at her, maintaining eye contact as she got closer and closer.

"Mr. Corbin?" she inquired with hard features and a modest smile.

The woman stood before me and I noticed the accessories along her waistline. A gold badge from the New Orleans Police Department sat atop her left side and she had a semi-automatic handgun holstered on her right. The word 'Detective' had been stenciled into the gold badge, and her authoritative demeanor made sense.

"Yes, I'm James Corbin," I replied, leaning back in my seat.

"I've been looking for you, sir. I have to thank your colleagues at your former place of work. Their descriptions of you were spot on. I'm

Detective Nola Maor of the New Orleans Police Department. Do you mind if we talk for a minute?"

"Sure. What is this about, Detective, and how did you know I would be here?"

"One of your former students' mothers is a colleague of mine. Her daughter, Chloe, recalled a discussion you had in your class about the fondness you have for this place. Chloe speaks highly of you, and your former colleagues also praised you, specifically for your knowledge of religion and religious history."

I paused, uncertain of how to react to my ex-colleagues' unexpected thoughts about me. It sounded as though they were complimentary. It would have been nice to hear those compliments when I still worked there.

"I thought they all hated me," I said in disbelief.

"Well, I'm afraid they also couldn't help but take some personal shots at you, especially, the principal, Dr. Wilson. She was not a very pleasant person. I dare say that she hates you," she revealed, averting her eyes with sympathy.

I nodded. "Of course, they did. I'm sure your assessment of Dr. Wilson's feelings toward me is accurate."

The feeling's mutual, I thought.

"Mr. Corbin, I'm not here to gossip with you about your former coworkers. I'm here because I'm hoping you can help me."

Detective Maor reached into the inner waistband of her pants and pulled out a small notepad.

An unusual place to keep a notepad, but practical.

The detective raised her hand toward Mrs. Redd and signaled for a fresh cup of coffee, turning back to me with a stern expression, as if trying to see through me.

As she stared at me, I took the time to admire her stunning features. Her smooth skin looked healthy, and her scent reminded me of the freshly-cut peaches my mother used to make for her cobbler. The nostalgic smell forced some unexpected memories of her, and I could hear my mother telling me to ask the detective out, but as attractive as she was, I had to pick her brain on what she wanted to know.

"*One True God,*" I interrupted.

"Why, yes? How did you — "

"I read the paper too, Detective. If you sought me out for my knowledge on religion and religious history, then it is rather obvious," I replied with confidence.

"Well, I want to know what type of person I might be dealing with here. What might his or her motive be for murdering innocent people?" Detective Maor questioned, tapping her pen on the table in frustration.

"I am not a criminal profiler, Detective, but I may be able to help you understand your suspect a little better. From the information leaks to the news media, I gathered that NOPD denied the possibility of a serial killer. I suspect everything reported was accurate? There are never signs of forced entry and the killer leaves a note that reads, *'One True God'* somewhere on the scene. The killings are execution style."

"I will not provide you with any details of the case, Mr. Corbin," the Detective said. "It's unfortunate that my colleagues leaked such things to the press. However, I will acknowledge that all the victims were strong religious figures in the community."

Mrs. Redd delivered the coffee to the table and presented a sly smirk in my direction after getting a better look at the detective. Detective Maor added a few packs of sweetener.

"Fair enough, Detective. I'll assume that the information leaked is accurate. Religious extremists can originate from any culture and religion. All that's needed are the right conditions. Generally, most people follow a religion because it provides comfort . An educated guess would be that your suspect has a painful history, and whatever their religion is now, they feel it requires their good works for repentance. It could be because they have a history of violence, a sense of worthlessness, or are simply a deviant that views their religion as absolute. They may believe in what they are doing," I explained, tapping the headline of the newspaper.

"Are you telling me this isn't some gimmick as an excuse to kill?" she huffed, taking another sip of her drink.

"Exactly. Their current religion has given them a sense of belonging, a purpose. Given their wording on the notes left behind, I would assume that their religion is Christianity, probably Catholicism given the city we are in, allowing them to fit right in. They could be looking for redemption, or they could believe they were chosen for a higher purpose. Either way, you are dealing with a determined and dangerous individual, or possibly a group of people. Of course, these are all assumptions, considering I have few details."

Detective Maor tilted her head. "A higher purpose?"

"Yes. Whether it is social rejection, mental illness, vindication, or simply a calling, society rejected this person and now they believe the secular government and laws no longer apply to them. They're hell bent on enforcing, *'Thou shall put no other god before me.'*"

The detective nodded. "Interesting. You have helped me more than you could understand, Mr. Corbin. I'm happy we had the chance to meet."

Detective Maor finished the last of her coffee and stood from the table.

I followed her actions, hoping to look into her hazel eyes for a few moments more. I enjoyed her company and wanted to stay in her presence for as long as possible.

"Tell me, Detective, what are you going to do about the bloodshed in this city? The thugs killing each other, *'One True God;'* and now, what is it called?"

"Goliath," she said, rolling her eyes. "We are doing all we can to put every single one of them behind bars. It's interesting that you referred to 'Goliath' as a 'what,' Mr. Corbin. A man of your education can't believe the rumors going around this city. There are enough problems and folklore in this city without worrying about ghosts and goblins. The murders are brutal, but I assure you that the suspect is human."

"I agree, Detective. I simply find the matter of the Goliath fascinating, brutal, and rather sad. Does NOPD have a suspect?"

"Mr. Corbin, I'm not here for the Goliath murders, and I have already stated that I will not provide you with details on ongoing cases, especially, one I did not consult with you. I already have your home and cell phone numbers provided by your former employer. I need to gather more information for your background check. I'll be in touch. As a matter of fact, here is my office number. Call me if you think of anything further that can help."

Detective Maor smiled and scribbled her number on a piece of paper from her notepad.

I frowned. "Wait, a background check? For what?"

"Standard on all paid consultants for NOPD, sir. Once I relay what you have given me, the ranking officials will want to get you on the payroll. Are you fine with that?" she asked.

"Sure. I've never considered it, but okay," I replied. My stomach twisted with unease.

I smiled as she nodded and left the coffee shop, and even with my newfound confidence, I still lacked the strength to ask her out.

But do I truly want another woman in my life after what Candace did? Could I handle the pain if everything went wrong again?

"Maybe next time."

CHAPTER
FIFTEEN

"There is no way I'm telling a soul about what I saw."
—Deputy Bailey

Another blazing hot summer night in Beauregard Parish had Deputy Bailey sweating buckets in his squad car, but he did not retreat to the relief of the air conditioning. That wasn't how soldiers behaved. The military had taught him to adapt to his environment, so he kept the car window down and listened to his surroundings; the engine idled in case of emergency. Besides, at this time of night in the suburbs, there was a still quiet, almost as if the parish was abandoned.

Like many nights before, Bailey parked his car and looked toward the train tracks, the landmark point that separated the two parishes.

"Only thirty minutes left before I can get my ass home and in my bed. I want to get as far away from New Orleans as I possibly can. What a cesspool," he mumbled, shaking his head as he looked over the parish line.

Deputy Bailey stared at the front page of the Beauregard Gazette, which lay on the passenger seat, and read the multiple headlines about the murder and carnage in New Orleans.

He glanced at the Iron Cross tattoo on his forearm and felt a sense of determination in his self-appointed mission.

"God damned animals. Entire city covered in blood. I won't let y'all infect my little slice of America," he spat.

Bailey had a quick look in his rearview mirror and noticed that the cross on top of the Catholic church was distorted and jagged. He leaned closer to get a better look, and his eyes widened with alarm. "What the hell is that?" he questioned. "Is that a person up there?"

Bailey spotted the bright glow of two vibrant yellow dots and the silhouette of long muscular limbs. His body ran cold with unease and his heartbeat quickened.

"What the fuck is that?" Deputy Bailey yelled again, jumping out of his squad car, and falling to his hands and knees.

Although he had spent most of his early years leaping out of patrol cars in one swift motion, he didn't have the same speed anymore. His fifty-year-old, overweight body would not allow it.

The sting of the hot concrete sent a shooting pain up his limbs, but he got to his feet and brushed himself down.

Leaving the car door ajar, Bailey looked up at the church rooftop and pulled his flashlight from its holster. He illuminated the rooftop with his torch and the figure sauntered in a catlike manner, as it leaped from the church to the top of the hardware store next door. Bailey tracked its movement along the rooftop and into the well-lit backdrop of the store's neon sign, but the sight of what stood above him sent feelings of panic through his body. His muscle memory failed him as he frantically patted around his gun belt in search for his firearm. His hands trembled with terror as he watched the beast stare at him with saber-like teeth.

"My God! It-it can't b-be?" Bailey stuttered, recalling what he read about a supposed creature that had killed four people last week.

Deputy Bailey raced back to his car as fast as he could; his feet uncoordinated as he tripped and collapsed onto the hot pavement once again. The flashlight slid toward the car and coins, keys, and other articles fell from his pockets. Bailey pulled himself off the pavement, grabbed the keys, and scurried back into his vehicle, but the beast vaulted from the rooftop and smashed into the passenger side door of his car, causing the vehicle to shutter from side to side.

His hands trembled and his breathing labored. Bailey slammed his foot on the gas pedal and caused his tires to spin and screech. White smoke saturated the air, but he managed to push off moments later. Bailey sped toward the sheriff's station, but the crushing sound of metal near the rear of the car followed him.

Only blocks away, Bailey rushed to the parking lot. His foot slammed the brakes as he parked the vehicle outside the station and rested his head upon the steering wheel. He breathed a sigh of relief as his hands continued to shake. Bailey quickly wiped his teary eyes, embarrassed by his cowardice, but relaxed at the thought of the deterrent the sheriff's station provided.

"There is no way I'm telling a soul about what I saw. How in the hell am I gonna explain this car?" he uttered to himself. His voice quivered as the stench of the burned rubber from the tires filled his stomach with nausea.

Deputy Bailey took several deep breaths, gathered himself, and hurried into the police station for a shift change. The cool air-conditioned building gave him a sense of safety and calmness, especially as he could now surround himself with a few fellow deputies.

As he hobbled up to the front desk, Bailey took a few more deep breaths, still not certain whether he imagined what he saw.

"Hey, Bailey. Another quiet night?" the desk sergeant asked; the same repetitive question he asked every other night.

"Yeah, Sarge. Nothing special," Bailey meekly replied.

"HEY, BAILEY!" a voiced yelled from the entrance.

Bailey jumped with a startled look and turned around. One of the new deputies strolled toward him.

"What the hell happened to your wheels? Did someone hit you?" the young deputy inquired.

Bailey's eyes widened, unsure what to say. "What are you talking about?"

"Um... the front passenger side door of your squad car. How could you not know? Come, take a look!"

Bailey followed the young deputy outside with the sergeant in toe, curious about the situation.

"What the fuck is this, Bailey?" the sergeant yelled, his face turning red with rage. "You told me it was another quiet night! How did you think you were going to hide this shit from me?"

Deputy Bailey pretended to inspect the side of the vehicle in fake disbelief. He could explain the door, but he could not explain the other damage without sounding crazy.

"Did you grind up against a fence or something?" the younger deputy asked.

Bailey stared at the damage, and his speechlessness, plus the fear, overwhelmed him.

The slashes on the car stretched from the rear passenger door all the way through the rear passenger side panel, and they looked exactly like claw marks to Bailey. He remembered the sound of crushing metal when he pulled off and his heart rate tripled.

"Goliath?" Bailey mumbled, feeling stupid.

Both the sergeant and the deputy guffawed at Bailey's response.

"Enough of your jokes, Bailey. This shit isn't funny. Look, this is your take-home car, so you are ultimately responsible for the damages. Go home and be sure to bring me a report that explains this in the morning. It better be good, or I might have to suspend your ass. You got me?" the sergeant ordered.

Deputy Bailey tuned out the sergeant's orders, as he scanned the rooftops of the adjacent buildings, terrified the beast may still be nearby.

"YOU GOT ME, BAILEY?" the sergeant yelled again, gaining Bailey's attention.

Bailey jumped at the sergeant's voice. "Sure, Sarge, I'll have it for you tomorrow."

Without hesitation, Bailey removed his gun belt and placed it into the trunk of his car. Nervously patting his pocket for his car keys, he realized he had lost both his flashlight and wallet when he fell. Bailey was overwhelmed with the urge to leave the station, so he could tell his wife what happened. It was enough to prevent him from going back to the scene to search for his belongings. He wasn't sure she would believe him, but he had to tell someone he trusted.

Gripped with fear, Deputy Bailey sped home the few miles from the sheriff's station.

Seconds after he pulled into the driveway of his middle-class home, Bailey looked over the area with haste.

On any other night, Bailey would take a moment to enjoy the ascetics of the confederate flag in the front of his home, but that night, he wasted no time and rushed inside.

"BARBARA!" Bailey shouted, darting into the tidy living room.

But his wife was nowhere to be seen; the silence was deafening.

"BARBARA!" Bailey bellowed once more, but again she didn't respond. "Why isn't she answering me? And why the hell are all the lights on in the damn house? It's 2 in the goddamn morning."

He continued to shout Barbara's name as he made his way through the house, but still, she didn't utter a word. Bailey's heart pounded as he approached the bottom of the stairs and looked up to the top floor.

"Did she fall asleep? She usually waits up for me," he said, sensing something wrong.

Bailey grabbed the wooden railing and climbed the staircase with caution.

As he reached the top floor, he peered down the narrow hallway that led to their bedroom. Unlike downstairs, all the lights were off, except a small gap of light shining through the bottom of the door.

"Barbara?" he called out again in a soft but desperate tone.

Bailey dashed into the silent bedroom and skimmed the surroundings.

Much like the rest of the house, the bedroom was spotless, but oddly, the bed was made, and Barbara's book lay on her nightstand, bookmark in place and undisturbed. Bailey expected to lay on his wife's chest as she slept, a normal occurrence for her, yet nothing was normal about tonight.

Bailey continued to scan the room, and a few moments later, he noticed the light emanating from the master bathroom; the door was slightly open.

"Honey?" Bailey called out again, his legs weak with fear.

His eyes widened as he thought the worst, and he edged closer to the bathroom. The deafening silence amplified his labored breaths and rapid heartbeat as he approached the door.

"She's probably just relaxin' in the tub," he reasoned.

The wet carpet squelched beneath his shoe. Bailey looked down to investigate what had caused the sound.

A pool of blood covered the sole of his black boot, sending a surge of horror and panic through his body. Bailey shoved open the door. violently damaging the wall behind it, and crumbled at the sight before him.

The severed head of his wife rested on its side, and her empty eyes glared back at him. Thick blood trickled down her pale face and her lifeless body laid still beside it.

Bailey's wallet had been placed open on the floor beside her, and her blood covered his driver's license.

The deputy's gut-wrenching pain caused him to collapse to his knees and scream in agony.

"No. No. No. No!" he cried, tears flowing down his chubby cheeks.

Bailey howled with an aching heart and clutched his chest as if he were embracing his wife, but a deep growl behind him caught his attention. His breathing shallowed and his brow curled with fear as he turned. Bailey looked over his shoulder and his whole being flooded with fright.

The monstrous beast with long canines and intense yellow irises stood in the bedroom behind him. Bailey froze as a stream of yellow fluid came down his leg and mixed with his wife's blood on the floor.

"Your terror ends here, Deputy. It's your time to suffer," Goliath snarled.

"No! Please, don't! What have we ever done to you?" Bailey pleaded.

His cries were ignored by the beast. Goliath extended his arm and ripped a gaping hole in Bailey's throat with his razor-sharp claws.

Blood poured from the new orifice; some splattered on the wall, and Bailey's heavy body hit the floor. The laughs of the beast were the last sound that fell upon his ears.

Goliath turned and smashed through the second story window, landing in the alleyway below as shattered glass fell from above. He sprinted away like a predatory jackal, hidden under the cover of darkness.

CHAPTER
SIXTEEN

*"They are God's servants, agents of wrath to bring punishment on
the wrongdoer."*—Detective Rossi

The nearby buildings in the block reflected the red and blue lights of
a passing police car on another summer night.

Detective Maor peered out the window in the bullpen office of
the First Precinct Investigative Unit and observed the stragglers from
Bourbon St. stumble their way from the French Quarter.

The late-night quiet of the office was the optimal off-duty place
to catch up on paperwork, but her mind weighed heavily on the
rampant murder activity in the city. Detective Maor's fingers tapped
the desk as she anticipated the long-distance call she had to make.

As she read over the two stacks of multiple incident reports
on her desk, she sighed at the sheer amount of work she had to get
through.

Damn it! I could use a little help here, she thought.

The pressure from the high-ranking brass and a lack of sleep had
affected Maor more than she thought possible. The stress she put on
herself to solve cases was far greater than any political pressure the
brass could apply.

Maor's leg quivered under the desk as she reanalyzed every
detail of her cases; from the witnesses twitching suspiciously, to the
suspects' tones and body language, but she couldn't focus as well as
normal. She continued to watch the ticking clock above the entrance,
eager to make her phone call.

These cases were all that mattered to the detective, but not for the reasons most cops have. Maor cared about what should matter to anyone who wore the badge. People were dying, and a murderer continued to prowl freely in the streets of New Orleans.

A colleague walked in; his radio amplified the voice of the silence wrecking dispatcher as both his and Maor's radios prompted. The young and athletically fit detective, still new to the investigative lifestyle, trudged into the office. His yawn was obnoxious, and his eyes were unusually red. His shoulders slouched before he sat, and his muscular arm pulled at his shirt.

His tie and the top button of his shirt were undone; no doubt to combat the constant heat of the night, but Maor didn't complain.

"Good morning, Jordan, long night?" Detective Maor asked.

"Yeah, we had three signal 30s tonight, likely retaliation and turf war shit between a bunch of young knuckleheads. We should be able to wrap this up when we apply a little pressure on the suspects," Jordan explained. "Nothing like what you are dealing with though. You trying to catch the worm again, huh, early bird?"

Maor admired his determination and positive mindset in these violent times. The city needed more of that attitude, and so did the department.

Maor glanced at Jordan from across the room and admired his powerful frame. He reminded her that it had been a while since she had some fun, but she preferred a man with a little more experience. Besides, fun with a colleague was a big no-no.

Maor lowered her head and returned her attention to a red suspect file on her desk.

She opened it and read the name written on the inside: *Nicholas Bianchi.*

Ever since she visited him at St. Mark's Church, she had tried to dig up as much information about Bianchi as possible, but her attempts had failed so far. Everyone associated with him had nothing but glowing things to say about him. but those positive job-like references from citizens and religious leaders in the community did not deter her. When she found a fellow officer in Rome, Bianchi's hometown, who could possibly shed some light on him, she had become anxious.

"Rome is 7 hours ahead, so she should be in by now," Maor mumbled, glancing at the clock.

She picked up the phone and dialed the number written in the red file, and she waved goodbye to Detective Jordan as it rang.

DESCENT OF A BROKEN MAN

"Polizia Municipale," a female voice answered in an Italian accent.

"Hi, um... hello. I didn't think this through enough. Do you speak English? I'm Detective Nola Maor of the New Orleans Police Department in America. Is there a Detective Gabriella Rossi there?" Detective Maor asked with awkwardness, tapping her pen on the desk.

"Speaking," the voice responded. "My lieutenant told me you would call this morning. Apparently, you have made a number of phone calls to various leaderships in a few different law enforcement departments here."

"Yes, I'm not one to take no for an answer with everything happening in my city," Maor said. "Well, if yours is the number they gave, maybe you are the one who can help me."

"Possibly," Rossi replied.

"Are you familiar with Deacon Nicholas Bianchi? Tall slender man, 6'2, well-kept and a tattoo of a torch on his right forearm," Maor questioned.

"No, I haven't had many encounters with clergy, despite living in Rome. I have —"

Maor dipped her brow at the silence on the other end. "Hello?"

"Yes, I-I'm h-here. I'm sorry; did you say a torch?" Rossi stammered.

"Yeah, a gold torch with a red flame. Four arching stars above it," Maor explained.

"I knew of a *David*, the suspect in one of my cases a few years back, but it can't be him. Well, I suppose it can be."

"Please, Detective Rossi, tell me about your cases," Maor pleaded.

"Si," she replied. "About five years ago, we had a series of execution-style murders committed by a group of individuals who had a singular motive — *The Cloth*. We found that they executed people based on the Ten Commandments of the Catholic religion. If they found that someone had violated them, they tied them up and slit their throats. A few were shot. Our task force later captured three of the perpetrators who were part of a prison gang called the Sons of Light. These were four individuals who were Christian extremists and believed God chose them to uphold his commandments here on Earth. They met in prison, and they all had a torch tattooed on their right forearm with four stars above the flame. We found that all three of the men that were captured had violent pasts and were steadfast in their cause. Unfortunately, we only apprehended three of the four

Sons. The fourth was never found, but we did get some information on who he was. His name was David, and he fits the description you provided, Detective. He slipped away from us, and we believe he fled the country. The prison he and his brothers were incarcerated in burned to the ground before their murderous spree, so we were never able to get his personal information to track him. We only managed to get a sketch of him. The other three only gave their purpose in the interviews. After that, none of them uttered a word," Rossi explained with a heavy sigh.

"Well," Maor said, "it appears that *David* found his way to New Orleans with a new name and title. We are having the same type of murders here, and from what I have deduced, they have the same religious motivation behind them. Not so much the Ten Commandments, but the worshiping of false gods. It's strange that these psychos commit murder to punish sin, which is a sin itself."

"Simply put, Detective, they do not believe that their actions are murder. They believe God chooses them. During my pursuit of the fourth suspect, I went to the burned prison, scavenging for something that could help us, and I found an etching on the wall in one of the charred cells of what was thought to be the fourth suspect. It gave me chills everywhere when I read it. It was Romans chapter 13, verse 4: *'For the one in authority is God's servant for your good. But if you do wrong, be afraid, for rulers do not bare the sword for no reason. They are God's servants, agents of wrath to bring punishment on the wrongdoer,'*" Rossi said.

"Interesting," Maor replied, monotone, but genuinely intrigued. She jotted the words of Rossi down as she spoke. "I was recently told something similar by an expert on religion here in New Orleans. It seems to me that religion causes more problems than it solves."

"I'm not sure that is accurate, Detective. Although I'm not a religious woman, I have seen it help more people find their way than not. Is there anything else I can help you with?" Rossi inquired.

"Yes. Can you fax me everything you have on David? The sketch you have would go a long way to help as well," Maor pressed.

"Absolutely. Detective, if your suspect *is* David, please don't underestimate him. He is a particularly violent man, and he's very smart. He managed to join and take over a prison gang in a matter of weeks, evade several law enforcement agencies, and flee the country. Most of all, he believes in his cause and will probably die for it as well. The sketch was provided to us by a witness who saw him driving in her neighborhood before one of their murders," Detective Rossi warned.

"Thank you, Detective Rossi. I look forward to your fax. Your info has been invaluable to me."

"Arrivederci, Detective. Good luck and God speed," Rossi said.

"Goodbye, Detective Rossi," Detective Maor replied, and hung up the phone.

Satisfied with how well her persistence paid off, Maor gathered her findings and exhaled as the room fell silent once again.

"The parallels between the murders are significant. The tattoo, the religious motivation, and the description of Rossi's fourth suspect fits," she said to herself.

As Detective Maor sorted through more of the details of the cases, looking for any evidence that could link to Deacon Bianchi, the intrusive sound of the fax machine violated her silence, but she looked over at the machine with glee as the papers slithered out.

"Wow! Already? Detective Rossi, you are truly a godsend!"

Maor ran over to the fax machine and grabbed the hand-drawn sketch from the tray.

"Son of a bitch! It's him!"

The black and white sketch showed a slightly younger Deacon Bianchi with much harder features and the same menacing look in his eyes.

"I've fucking got you, you murderous son of a bitch! Now I just have to prove it."

CHAPTER
SEVENTEEN

"I appreciate the offer, but I'm not interested."
—Detective Maor

As I strolled along the pristine pathway of the uptown university square, I felt the best I had in many years, and the effort I had placed into my everyday clothing had been reminiscent of my younger college days. My new square-toe shoes, pressed slacks, and shirt with a colorful tie was a distant cry from the dull browns I had settled into before. The late August heat could not deter me from choosing to always look my best these days, and I looked forward to the fall that would provide much cooler days and nights. Completely in the moment, I smiled as I reflected on my journey to get here.

"James, it's a pleasure to see you again," Dean Henton said. His face presented a rather large smile.

"It's a pleasure to be here, Dean. I've been waiting for this opportunity for quite a while," I said. The comfort of the chair was a welcome relief after the long walk across the university's grounds.

"I must admit, James, I was sure only a few weeks ago I wouldn't have considered bringing you aboard, let alone giving you an interview. I didn't feel you had the potential to be an asset to the History Department or the university. Now we are here in an informal interview because my decision is mostly made. Life can be strange." Dean Henton shook his head as he leaned back in his chair behind the rather large desk in his office.

"Yes, very strange, Dean," I replied. The uncontrollable thought

of eviscerating him flashed in my head.

"Two publications and a spot as a city consultant helping them solve these brutal murders in the city put you on our radar, Mr. Corbin. The fact that NOPD came to you first before consulting this university is a testament to your rather new reputation. I am curious about something though. When we spoke at the conference, you were working on research dealing with the supernatural elements of the Persian Empire. I noticed that wasn't one of your papers that were published. Did you not find the missing pieces you were looking for to prove your theory?"

I smiled as I stared at him, shifting in my chair. "I'm still working on finding more evidence. I do think what I find will be a game changer in the historian community, and if I'm a part of your faculty, for this university." Images of spilling his blood still flooded my head. I cleared my throat several times, unable to prevent the reoccurrence. "Why do you ask?"

"The thoughts of this so-called beast terrorizing the city. I've heard about its brutality and the rumors of what it looks like. I'm not sure what to believe, but the possibility of something like that existing — It terrifies me. It's making me believe that there may be more out there we don't understand."

He shuffled the random papers around on his desk, avoiding eye contact.

"I'm not sure there is some beast running around the city killing people, Dean. However, if that is the case, maybe we brought this hell down upon ourselves. Maybe it's time for everyone in this city to pay for their sins."

"U-um, yes. Interesting. Well, as I said before, this was very informal. We wanted to give you the opportunity to be a part of our faculty. We are offering our basic package for new educators, but the opportunity to continue to build both your pay and reputation with the help of our resources here are among the best in the nation. Are you still interested?"

"Absolutely!"

What a difference a month makes, I thought. The laughter of some nearby students helped me refocus.

"What's up, Professor Corbin? That a new whip?" a student asked as I approached my car.

I nodded in acknowledgement with a prideful grin on my face and proceeded to drive off the campus, reflecting on my new professorship at the university, the many consultation jobs with the

DESCENT OF A BROKEN MAN

NOPD, and hopefully the FBI, thanks to Nola's contact. Most men my age with newfound income would purchase a shiny sports car, but not me. I preferred the easy, gentle ride of a luxury sedan.

"Thank you, Ahriman," I said with gratitude. "Thank you for holding up your end. It feels good not to be forgotten for a change."

With gratefulness in mind, I considered calling Detective Maor to thank her for the recommendations again, but I wanted to thank her properly with a candle-lit dinner and maybe a dance. The thought of her lips pressed against mine helped with some of the still painful heartbreak from Candace.

I turned on the car radio and blared some of the popular music of the summer. It seemed I wasn't the only one in a vibrant mood as the streets were active with people and music.

The sights and sounds that surrounded me made for a pleasurable drive along St. Charles Ave., but the sudden news break interrupted the cheerful vibe in my car.

"The top of the hour news break is brought to you by our sponsors following this broadcast. New Orleans is still marred in murder with six more shootings yesterday, bringing the city's total to 337 murders over the last eight months. Detectives say the investigations from last night are ongoing, and the two active serial killers account for 21 of those killed. The 'One True God' killer is said to be responsible for eight of these victims, and the killer known as 'Goliath' accounts for an unbelievable 13. Although the NOPD denies the existence of Goliath, witnesses who claimed to see the monster still come forward and openly speak with news media. NOPD Superintendent (John) Roberts only had one comment on the matter. He stated that, 'All investigations are ongoing, although we expect to have the 'One True God' suspect in custody soon. NOPD is not interested in tales of ghosts and goblins regarding the so-called Goliath. The brutal murders being attributed to 'Goliath' are nothing more than the depraved and evil acts of one or more individuals who will be brought to justice shortly.'

"This is Sarah Hebert, 109.2 FM news."

The obnoxious commercials that followed the broadcast pushed me to lower the volume of the radio, and a mixture of conflicted emotions filled my heart. Part of me felt a sense of vanity that the beast had been mentioned in the broadcast, but I also felt sorrow at both the shootings and the killer on the loose.

"Your body count is crass, and you talk about these numbers as if no families got crushed as a result of these deaths. Killing for such trivial reasons is disgusting!" I barked at the radio as if it could hear me, but I soon winced at my hypocrisy and tried to reason with myself. "My situation is unique. I have a debt to pay, and blood is the price. I have to pay in full."

Unsure of whether to believe my own words, I parked outside the Crescent Moon Brewery, my new favorite social hangout in the city.

The outdoor craft beer spot provided a well-lit atmosphere with the most comfortable seating, and the indoor bar area was always air-conditioned for the heat-adverse patrons. The selection of flavored brews, paintings by a variety of local artists, and boundless food choices was enough to attract a wide span of customers. The diverse mixture of rich and middle classes, black and white alike, provided a rich social gathering for every day of the week.

The smell of freshly-brewed hops enticed me and my craving for the ice-cold suds from the bar won me over.

"Hey, James! How's it going, baby?" the young bartender greeted me in a flirty tone.

Her red hair complemented her emerald-green eyes, enlarged by her framed glasses that sat on her nose. Her tattooed arms suited her voluptuous figure and nerdy personality.

"Hey, Jessica. Do you mind if I use your phone?" I asked, disregarding her question. Jessica's smile dropped and she handed me the cordless phone from behind the bar.

"Thanks, Jessi," I said with an appreciative grin.

"Any time," she answered, winking at me.

I pulled a piece of paper from my shirt pocket and dialed the number written on the front.

The phone rang and my heartbeat tripled with anticipation. I wiped my sweaty palms on the side of my pants and took a deep breath to settle myself.

"First Precinct Investigations. This is Detective Maor," the voice answered.

"Hey, Detective. This is James Corbin. How are you?" I asked confidently.

Maor cleared her throat. "Hello, Mr. Corbin. This is a pleasant surprise. How can I help you?"

"How is the investigation going? Are you any closer to catching your man?"

"Mr. Corbin, I remember telling you this twice when we first met. I will not discuss the details of any active investigation regardless of your consulting status, sir," she replied in an assertive tone. "Now, what can I help you with?"

My stomach twinged with disappointment, but I continued.

"I know you've been working hard on your cases, so I wondered if you would like to meet me for a drink or two to take your mind away from your worries. Maybe after I can treat you to some dinner? A place of your choosing, of course," I inquired.

A prolonged silence ensued on the other end and my hands trembled with a mixture of nervousness and embarrassment. Maor and I had only met once, but when she gave me her phone number, I assumed she had more than consulting purposes in mind. However, the endless silence on the other end did not give me much hope.

"James, can I call you James?"

"Of course," I said, trying to smile through my anticipated disappointment.

"James, I appreciate the offer, but I'm not interested. Maybe some other time," she replied, and the phone fell silent again.

My heart sank at Maor's rejection, and I wondered how I could have been so wrong. I scanned the room with humiliation only to see Jessica staring at me with pity.

After I hung up the phone without another word, she slid a glass of my favorite brew in front of me.

I nodded with appreciation and glanced around at everyone smiling and laughing with friends and partners. Maor turning me down had been my first loss since the blessing of Ahriman, until the familiar sight of a woman at the other end of the bar caused me to pause.

Her shoulder-length hair as black as the night swayed around her face as her obnoxious cackle pierced the room. Her dark eyes were filled with joy, and her hand touched the accompanying man beside her. The sight of her caused me to forget about Maor's unfortunate rejection.

"Candace!" I shouted across the room, and I got up to walk toward her.

Candace looked up from the bar and her laughter stopped abruptly when she noticed me.

"Well, hello, Candace. How have you been?" I asked, glaring into her eyes, refusing to shy away from the immediate tension between us.

"I've been just fine, James," she answered, furrowing her brow with confusion.

Candace folded her arms in defense, but her eyes canvassed me from head to toe, as if she tried to figure out what had changed about me.

"I see you've upgraded your look. I didn't know Dress for Less sold those types of clothes," Candace hissed when she saw my new style. "I'm sure you know City Councilman, Phillip Lester?"

"Ah, yes. I'm familiar with the name. It's a pleasure to meet you, Councilman. I've heard that one day soon you'll be the mayor of this great city and possibly even governor," I said, shaking the councilman's hand.

"Governor? I'm not sure about that. I'm still a black man in the state of Louisiana. This state has never had an African-American governor, but I guess you never know," Phillip mused. "I've heard a lot about you, James. You're a high school history teacher, is that right?"

"Actually, no. I'm a professor at the university uptown. I'm also a consultant for NOPD and the FBI. I've had two papers published this month alone and I'm currently working on my first book... Phillip," I bragged, with a smug smile.

Candace's open mouth filled me with satisfaction, and Phillip dipped his brow as if I had just contradicted the information he had about me.

"Well, James, I see you've turned things around for yourself," Candace stated with the same tone of contempt. "It's nice to see you've accomplished something in your worthless life. Let me guess, no woman in your life, right?"

"Well, no. But I — "

Candace scoffed. "Typical, same self-absorbed James. You won't make it far and everything you've earned will fall apart. Just like you. You aren't built for success. Someone will take it from you. You're too soft! Slightly capable, but soft. This man, James, he isn't soft. He makes things happen without being miserable all the time for no reason!"

Candace smiled with bitterness after her tirade, and Phillip laughed in the background, turning his head to order another craft beer.

I continued to stare Candace in the eyes with an uncomfortable grin, and she glowered back, brimming with pride and certain that she still had the ability to hurt me.

"Apparently, you two are made for each other. It's been nice seeing you again, Candace. I hope you and the councilman get everything you deserve," I said calmly.

A subtle glow of bright yellow resonated in my eyes.

DESCENT OF A BROKEN MAN

Candace tilted her head, unsure of what she had noticed in my eyes, and her mouth hung ajar.

I strolled to the other end of the bar and ordered another one of my favorite craft beers. Jessica resumed her flirtatious routine with me again. I continued to watch Candace and the councilman from afar, but the sight of her happiness did not sit right with me.

As dusk set in, my mind drifted to thoughts of anger and blood. The taste of the beer became repugnant, and the sound of laughter and joyous conversation filled me with irritation. I no longer felt the comfort of the air conditioning, and the smell of Candace's flesh taunted me. Even on the other end of the bar, its sweet stench forced me outside.

I returned to my parked car and observed the patrons who came out one by one, all at different levels of boisterous intoxication. Candace and Phillip exited the brewery after their happy hour indulgence and stopped to passionately kiss each other at the front entrance. She wrapped her arms around his back, and he grabbed her ass with his large hands.

My blood boiled at their affection, and heat rose from my skin. Sweat saturated my body, and my transformation began. Candace and Phillip stumbled toward her car and slumped into the seats.

"Let's go home, big boy, so I can take advantage of you," I heard Candace yell with my heightened hearing. I followed them from a distance and listened to her unconfined laughter from their car. The sight of another man intimately engaging with my wife made me want to ensure that he never put his hands on her again.

As I continued to follow, the recollection of Candace berating and abandoning me enraged me, inducing the final stages of my transformation. The chilling thought of spilling their blood filled me with a burning desire, and as triangular teeth extended over my protruding jaw, everything went dark.

I stood on my clawed feet; clothes shredded from the violence of the change. I let out a ferocious roar as I chased Candace's car, leaping from rooftop to rooftop, as I listened to them talk and tracked the scent of their sweat soaked flesh.

The smell of the alcohol permeating from Phillip's skin, mixed with the scent of Candace's perfume tempted me as I tracked Candace's car through the Seventeenth Ward neighborhood.

ASHON RUFFINS

"W-why are you taking us this way, babe? I hate the Seventeenth and... it's getting darker," Phillip slurred.

"There is always a street party going on around here. I'm feeling it right now and I wanna shake my ass," Candace said, as the car accelerated.

"Well, if we are going this way, let me get my shit ready."

"Is that really necessary? You'd think you were compensating for something carrying that big ass thing around. Then again, I love a man being a man."

The sound of a moan was evident in the car and my rage pushed me faster across the roof of houses to keep pace; my claws sliced through shingles and a trail of debris was left behind.

Farther down the road, Candace slowed the car near what looked like an impromptu block party. The repetitive beat of the bounce music blared from towering speakers as dozens of people danced in the street. The thick crowd had swallowed the road and made it their personal dance floor.

Candace stopped the car in the middle of the street. As I watched her hop out to dance, a smile fell upon Phillip's face as he eyed her hips swaying to the rhythm. He tucked the gun into his waistband and exited the car.

The cheerful party, the music, and the dancing attracted dozens of people as I peered on and watched them enjoy the atmosphere. I couldn't wait any longer. The sight of Candace's smile, the joy she had; I wanted to end it in the most tortuous way possible.

As the gathering continued, I jumped from the rooftop of a nearby home. My massive arms extended, and knees folded into my chest; the power allowed me to be in complete control, and perfectly designed to hunt.

The deafening *thump* on Phillip's car as I landed shattered the windows and sent shards of glass into the crowd. The alarm blared, and everyone at the party turned their heads and surrendered their attention to the vehicle.

"What the fuck is that?" Candace screamed. Her eyes widened.

I stood, my full beastly figure on display, as everybody screamed into the night air and fled.

Phillip and Candace covered their heads with fear as they were paralyzed with terror.

I skulked down the front of the car; my claws ripped through the fiberglass hood as if it were paper. The front end of the Mercedes crumpled under the weight, only for the front end to snap back up

114

violently, causing the alarm to die.

I towered before Candace, bared teeth, and growled with pleasure as she cowered. She looked into my yellow eyes, as I slowly moved closer; the rancid breath hit her face. Candace belted out a screech that echoed in the night and trembled with complete terror. A few intrigued witnesses cowered in disbelief at the sight of my bloodthirsty presence.

Although blood trickled from the many cuts on Phillip's face caused by the flying shards of glass, he found the courage to grab his gun from his waist and fired a shot at the monstrous figure before him.

A bullet pierced my right shoulder, which only caused me to laugh at his pathetic attempt. Phillip fired his weapon several more times, hitting me in the chest, as I launched toward him and clutched his throat. My claws squeezed his neck and lifted him off the ground. The gun fell from his grasp and slid across the pavement.

I growled again with pleasure as his legs struggled to find the ground. I glared at Candace as the discharged rounds fell from my skin. The thunderous roar reverberated throughout Candace's body, as I tore out the flesh from the councilman's throat. Phillip's body hit the concrete and blood poured from the gaping hole in his neck. His mouth twitched as he gasped for air like a fish out of water; his eyes were wide and packed with fear as he fixed them on Candace.

But after a few moments, his body went still.

Candace screamed as tears fell from her eyes and I slowly prowled toward her.

"Too soft," I growled, staring at Candace. I wrapped my large claw around her jaw and sliced her cheek with one of my sharp nails.

Candace fell to her knees, terrified and bawling uncontrollably.

"Typical," I said as I turned and fled the scene.

In the distance, the sound of sirens drew closer, while everyone stood around and stared in terror and disbelief, while I took pleasure and watched from a nearby rooftop.

Candace lay on the pavement, exhausted with fear.

"Phillip, no. Oh, God. Please, no." Tears flowed from her eyes and blood poured down her cheek.

CHAPTER EIGHTEEN

"Signal 30, Code 2, 2300 block of Jackson Ave."
—NOPD Dispatcher

The soothing hum of the idle car engine harmonized with the air conditioning that kept Detective Maor cool and comfortable. It had only been a few hours, but the patience it took for her to sit in one place and do nothing had never been one of her strengths.

"I passed up a drink with a cute guy for this?" Maor asked herself, unsure if she was more interested in the drink or the phone call from James right now. "At least he had the guts to call. Ugh, it's been so long. The way he hung up the phone though... shit, James is a confident guy. He'll call back. Nola! You're talking to yourself again."

The random crackles of the police radio briefly interrupted her one-sided conversation.

"God, I need a drink," she said as she glanced at the vodka on the floor, but she refocused on her sights through the binoculars. "Another book!" Detective Maor yelled in frustration. "This guy is more of a bookworm than me!"

As she continued to watch, her lips tensed and her brow furrowed. The cool confines of the car suddenly made her feel cramped.

Although she kept her home spotless, the passenger seat and floor were littered with empty pastry wrappers, bags of potato chips, and empty water bottles.

"Four hours and he hasn't even stepped outside! Just sits in that chair with his nose in a book. C'mon, Deacon," Maor mumbled. "No human being is this robotic. Not even to go to the bathroom?"

The murder suspects she had been accustomed to chasing did not move with the patience and discipline of Bianchi. Their sloppy crimes were usually done out of anger without much of a plan, but Bianchi had not moved for hours.

The police radio's beep grabbed Maor's attention, diverting her focus away from Deacon Bianchi.

"Signal 30, Code 2, 2300 block of Jackson Ave. Suspect has fled the scene. Dozens of witnesses are waiting on scene to speak with police."

Maor raised her brow in shock. "Ma'am, did I hear that right? Dozens of witnesses *want* to talk to the police?"

The radio beeped again as the dispatcher continued to air more information. "Umm... I'm not sure if this is correct, but witnesses are saying... witnesses stated Goliath committed the murder. Witnesses also stated that it... oh my God... it ripped out the victim's throat! Hold on. Wait. The victim... the victim is Councilman Phillip Lester. All units, Code 3. Emergency Services are en route!"

Detective Maor stared at her handheld radio in disbelief and tossed it onto her passenger seat.

"DAMN IT! Next time, Deacon!" she yelled in frustration. Her foot slammed on the accelerator as she drove to the new crime scene.

The sound of the screeching tires echoed throughout the narrow street and caused Deacon Bianchi to peer out his window and smile at the detective's absence.

He placed his book onto the table beside him and turned off the light. Bianchi ambled to his bedroom and opened the closet to see a black shoe box on the floor. A disturbing grin covered his face as he prepared to take advantage of the detective's leave.

"It's time to do God's work."

CHAPTER NINETEEN

"I had to take care of some unfinished business tonight."
—James Corbin

My speed from the alleyway would be considered reckless, but the distance covered from uptown, over the industrial canal and back into the lower Ninth Ward in only fifteen minutes, would be considered a record in some circles. After I pulled up outside Priestess Nadia's house and cut the engine, I leaned back, shirtless, with blood spattered across my arms and bare chest.

Oddly, the sight of it made me uncomfortable, and I felt worse when I reflected on what happened.

I rubbed the fresh cuts in the passenger side seat and promised myself never to transform in the new car again. I didn't want to attract attention to myself more so than I did when Goliath took over me.

Transforming into Goliath always gave me an addictive rush of power, but each time I turned back to myself, the rush became less and less compared to the first time.

I had spilled blood for Ahriman, and I enjoyed doing it, but not like the first time when I killed Damon and Cynthia in Armstrong Park. There was no conflict.

I sighed and stared at Nadia's little Voodoo shop before me, uncertain of what had brought me there, instead of the comfort of my home after what I had done. However, I often found myself at Nadia's when I needed someone to talk to, so I assumed my instinct pushed me there. The shop had always provided a sanctuary, especially on the days I struggled the most.

The clock on my dashboard read 10:34 p.m.; early enough to not worry about being an unexpected burden, but in no way could Nadia see me covered in blood and dirt.

I exited the car and grabbed my backup bag full of fresh clothes and towels from the trunk; I had learned to keep it on me in case I wanted to go unnoticed after the transformation.

After I changed in the back seat, I used a bottle of water and an old towel to wipe the blood from my skin.

I shoved it all back into the trunk and made my way into Nadia's place, as I climbed the stairs and opened the door.

"Priestess, are you here?" I called out with a smile on my face.

Like every time I had visited before, Priestess Nadia relaxed in her normal spot at the far end of the room; the perfect place for her to gaze out the window and fulfill her role as the watchful gatekeeper of her beloved neighborhood.

The old tabletop radio played contemporary jazz music in the background, and the scent of burned roses permeated throughout the room from the incense.

"James, this is a surprise. What brings you here tonight?" Nadia asked in a manner that suggested my arrival did not surprise her.

"I had to take care of some unfinished business tonight, which made me think of you," I said evasively.

"I'm sure, James. You've been a busy man, haven't you?" she stated. Her lips barely raised as she gave me an unenthusiastic grin.

I tilted my head and squinted my eyes. "I'm sorry?"

"Well, the last time we spoke, you weren't doing so well. You were in a dark place, and your light was gone. Did you ever talk to someone like I suggested, baby?" she asked.

"No, ma'am, I —"

"The only thing that made you smile that night was the book you found here."

"Book?" I said, playing dumb.

"Yes, James, the old text on Zorothorism. You wanted it for your research. Although, I had no idea it was here. It manifested itself here like so many other artifacts. Usually, I can sense when something new arrives, but not that time. It found you anyway. You're the one it must have been looking for," she said.

How did she know the book was about Zorothorism? Had she been keeping something from me? Did she know what I had done? I wondered.

DESCENT OF A BROKEN MAN

I stared at the Priestess in response, aware that she fished for information.

"Yes, ma'am, the book was insightful. I am lucky to have found it as it has opened doors in my research and shed light on what I missed before."

"Doors? Ah, I see," she said, as she grabbed that creepy walking cane of hers. "James, you seem different. *Changed.* Your new car outside tells me that you've had some professional success recently, but you, the James I know — your aura doesn't appear as bright as usual. Your light is dim and it seems to be getting darker. Exactly what doors did that book open for you?"

"You're right!" I barked, angered by her assertion. "That pathetic excuse for a black man is gone. There is no more weakness. I can't be weak, not in this country. Not in this state and not in this city. No woman wants a weak man. There is no room for depression. It was eating me alive, so I got rid of it! Now I'm the one doing the eating!"

The Priestess glared at me. Her face covered in disappointment at my arrogant display of pride. "You sound foolish. So, what exactly are you eating?"

Before I could answer Priestess Nadia, the radio blasted a news update into the room.

"We have breaking news this evening. Councilman Phillip Lester of the Eighth District was murdered uptown tonight, while partaking in an impromptu block party. Councilman Lester was fatally wounded by what witnesses are saying was the murderous beast known as Goliath. It seems there are dozens of witnesses to corroborate the sighting. If eyewitness reports are true, there is something nefarious in the streets of New Orleans. Once again, Councilman Phillip Lester has been murdered tonight by what witnesses have reported to be the beast Goliath. This is a little hard to believe, but we'll have more information tonight as details unfold. This is Nancy Allen, WKOL AM radio!"

The voice over the radio silenced and the jazz music continued. Priestess Nadia paused with fright; her eyes widened as she turned back to me.

"James! What have you done?" she yelled. "It was the book, wasn't it? What evil have you manifested? What was in that book, young man?"

Nadia's barrage of questions caught me off guard, but I stared at her without a measure of regret. I turned my head toward the mirror on the adjacent wall, but my reflection looked unfamiliar. My features were hardened and more rigid, and the flesh around my eyes had sunken as if I had indulged in illegal substances.

"It's too late for me, Nadia. What's done is done. Besides, your shop did exactly what you said it's here for, to put me on my path," I said.

"It's never too late. It's never too late to seek help! Whatever evil you have conjured, we can figure it out. We can reverse it."

Still unable to look her in the eyes, I turned and walked back to the door, but I paused and stared at the floorboards.

"I'm afraid it's too late for me. The more I change, the less of me comes back. I like the power. I love the rewards. It's worth it to me. You have always been a good friend to me, Nadia. Thank you," I told her, without looking back.

I hurried back to my car, anxious to get home, when the headlights of an approaching vehicle blinded me. The driver's pale skin stuck out like a sore thumb as I watched him turn the corner.

"Another white guy who has no idea what neighborhood he wandered into. Tourists can be pretty stupid," I scoffed.

As I started the car, Nadia hobbled out of her shop and staggered toward my window.

"James, let me help you!" she shouted, breaking the silence of the tranquil neighborhood, but I yanked my vehicle into drive and sped away.

CHAPTER TWENTY

"What do you want, you coward?"
—Priestess Nadia

Priestess Nadia watched James drive away and wondered if she would see her friend again. She sighed as she scanned the quiet neighborhood, relieved that she hadn't disturbed any of her neighbors, but as she ambled back into her home, sorrow overwhelmed her. She thought about the desperate actions of her lost friend, but there was nothing she could do to save him. Nadia knew James would eventually have found himself on this path, regardless of his intelligence or life choices. She knew James' pain and desperation would consume him.

She closed the door behind her with a low head and mumbled one word.

"Ahriman."

Chills and goosebumps covered her frail body as the word eased from her lips. She tottered back to her chair to get comfortable and jotted down James' name in her visitor's log journal as she had done so many times before. Nadia peered out the window; her eyes widened at the figure in the front yard. This time her hand was not as steady when she jotted down the name of the figure she saw before he knocked on her door. She jumped at the sound of the intense knocking that shook the door violently.

Nadia shuffled back to the door in an attempt to put the latch in place, when a familiar face opened the door and greeted her with a sinister smile on the other side.

"What the hell are you doing here?!" she exclaimed.

"Hell, Priestess? Not Hell, *Heaven*," Deacon Bianchi replied in an icy tone.

He placed his hands on Priestess Nadia's chest and shoved her to the floor, knocking over the shelving and most of the novelty items in the store. Deacon Bianchi sauntered inside and pulled a gun from his waistband, not forgetting to lock the door behind him.

"Now Priestess, it's time we revisit our earlier conversation," Bianchi stated as he pointed the nickel-plated revolver at her head. "Please, madam, let me help you up."

Bianchi reached out with his other hand, but Nadia pushed it away, refusing any help from her abuser. She slowly climbed to her feet, her old bones weary, and once again stood before him with a twisted grimace of disgust on her face.

"What do you want, you coward?" she asked, as she wiped the blood from her lip.

"In due time, idolator. First, turn around and place your hands behind your back," Bianchi ordered.

Nadia turned with reluctance and Bianchi tightly bounded her wrists behind her back with the plastic zip ties he retrieved from his pocket.

"Who's the man who just left? A little young for you, don't you think, Priestess?" he asked.

"Don't be crass! Unfortunately, he's another lost and misguided soul, like yourself. As I told you on your last visit, I help others find their paths."

"Ah, yes, through your so-called *religion*," Bianchi mocked. "Well, Priestess, oddly enough, your religion is our topic of discussion again."

Bianchi struck her across her face with the butt of his gun and Nadia fell to the floor once again.

"On your knees!" he bellowed, forcing her into a position he had put others into many times before.

Bianchi looked down at Nadia and smiled, relishing in her obvious discomfort as her bare knees pressed on the hardwood floor.

"Comfortable?" he taunted. "Priestess, you have spent your days manipulating others away from our Lord, filling their heads with unnatural forces to help guide them through their troubles. It's perversion of the soul and an affront to God. Your ways are wicked, and it leads other souls to hell, as well as your own. You need to repent!"

Nadia stared up at Bianchi, unwilling to show the intense pain from kneeling on the unforgiving wooden floor.

DESCENT OF A BROKEN MAN

"Typical," she spat.

"Excuse me?" he replied, pressing the tip of the gun against her forehead. "Do you have something to say, you piece of trash?"

"You heard me!" she retorted. "I've seen your type too many times. Nut bags like you are more interested in following rules than the enlightenment of the soul. You aren't saving anyone. Even worse, you are a perversion of what the Catholic religion teaches. You're pathetic."

"Signora, I am ordained by God to remove the weeds that suffocate his garden of salvation," Bianchi lectured, stepping back to maintain his composure.

Nadia's words filled him with rage, and he tried to remain calm as a familiar object on a display table in the corner caught his attention.

Its smooth design and bone handle were as attractive as the first time he had spotted it, and he couldn't help but wander over to pick it up. Bianchi's fingers caressed the handle as he admired his reflection in the steel blade. The reflection of his dead eyes stared back at him, and his connection to the handcrafted weapon was like nothing he had ever felt before.

"Priestess, you were right about this blade. It is quite comfortable in my hands. That's another conversation; though I am afraid your time has come to an end." Bianchi resumed his place behind Nadia with a look of bloodlust in his eyes.

"Romans 1:18: *For the wrath of God is revealed from heaven against all ungodliness and unrighteousness of men who suppress the truth in unrighteousness,*" he recited as he lifted the blade from his side.

In one quick motion, Bianchi slashed the blade across Priestess Nadia's throat, causing her to choke and gasp for air. Her body crumpled onto the hard floor and Bianchi watched the thick blood pour from the wound and the light left her sweet eyes.

"I hope you find forgiveness in the afterlife, Priestess. Your judgment has been rendered."

Deacon Bianchi pulled a small, clean painter's brush from his pocket and kneeled beside Nadia's lifeless body. He smiled as his barbaric actions gave him a sense of accomplishment and pride.

The upbeat jazz music from the radio filled the room as Nadia's blood soaked into the imperfections of the wooden floor.

He grinned at the bloody note by her body as he tucked the blade away under his clothing.

'One True God.'

CHAPTER TWENTY-ONE

"We saw the party, and I wanted to stop."
—Candace Corbin

The whimpers and sobs from dozens of individuals in the background made Detective Maor uncomfortable. The sight of so many uniforms taking statements had become the norm to her over the years, but the slaughter of a public servant and the sighting of a monster had changed things.

However, Maor had not provided a suspect for the murders taking place in the city, so the death of Phillip Lester could put her in the political hot seat. Her prowess and skill as an investigator had earned her this position, but if she weren't careful, these surreal cases could make her the fall guy.

Maor stared at the lifeless body of the councilman and observed the immediate surroundings. The weapon and spent casings on the ground confirmed the witnesses' statements about the gunfire, and Maor began to wonder whether the tall tale about Goliath may not have been so tall after all.

She closed her eyes and reenacted the scene in her head the best she could, trying to picture what may have happened. The images in her head played as if she was there to witness it herself.

"He was able to pull his weapon and fire four shots at close range," Detective Maor mumbled. "I don't see any other trauma, so only someone with considerable strength could have left a fatal wound that size. Twenty-seven witnesses. *Twenty-seven,* all giving the same description."

Maor approached the squad car and noticed another tearful witness inside, repeatedly wiping her face. She opened the door, and the woman inside turned and looked in her direction.

A large bandage covered a fresh wound on her right cheek.

"Hi. I'm Detective Maor of the NOPD. Can I ask your name?"

"I'm Candace," she stated, wincing from the pain in her jaw.

Maor nodded and said, "Candace, can you tell me what happened here?"

"I'm...I'm not sure. I mean, I have no idea whether that *thing* was real. It must have been. Everyone screamed at the sight of it, and... and Phillip tried to shoot it, but the bullets didn't hurt it. My God, it ripped out his throat! How is that possible?" she explained, her voice breaking with every word.

"Candace, you called the attacker an 'it.' Did you get a good look at the person? Was it a man? Can you describe him?" Detective Maor asked, trying to get Candace to see sense and pin the horrific act on a human being.

An investigator asking multiple questions all at once was a tactical error when it came to interview and interrogation techniques, but Maor needed answers fast.

"We saw the party, so we got out of the car and danced for a while. It fell out of the sky and landed on top of the car!" Candace said.

Detective Maor turned and inspected the damaged car. The top had been completely caved in and large animal size paw prints and claw marks were indented into the roof, as if something had crushed it. Every window had been shattered and pieces of broken glass surrounded the vehicle.

"It went after Phillip. Its skin looked like old, cracked leather, coarse and scarred, and its teeth were large like a big cat," Candace added.

"How big was it?" Maor questioned, with no choice but to entertain the idea.

"Well, it picked Phillip up with one arm, and Phillip isn't...wasn't small. It... stared at me while it held him up above its head, and... smiled as if it enjoyed killing him."

Maor's eyes widened. "It smiled at you?!"

"And spoke," Candace added. "I think it said, '*too soft*', which is odd, because those are the words I said to my husband earlier this evening."

"Wait! I'm sorry. Your husband? Has anyone called him?" Maor asked.

"No. I hate him! Listen to me!" Candace yelled. "After it killed Phillip, it came over to me and cut me with its hideous claws. But its eyes... its eyes were yellow and evil and... familiar. I knew them. They reminded me of my husband's eyes, but this thing wasn't human. It seemed happy to terrorize me... happy to cause me pain. After that, it ran."

Detective Maor shook her head in disbelief. Not *everyone* could be mistaken.

"It appears monsters are real," Maor said as a shiver came over her.

Candace's eyes widened at her words.

The overwhelming feeling of fear that passed through her made her legs feel like jelly, but she couldn't show weakness in front of the victims who needed help.

"Candace, what is your last name? Is there anyone we can call to pick you up?" Maor asked.

"You can call my mother. My last name is Corbin. Candace Corbin. I know, it sounds like a bad comic book character," she said, stroking the bandage taped to the side of her face.

Maor furrowed her brow at the name Corbin, but she couldn't immediately place where she had heard it before. She wanted to pause and think, but she had to prioritize the situation at hand.

"Officer! Please see Mrs. Corbin to the station and help her get in contact with her mother," Detective Maor ordered.

"Yes, Detective," the officer replied from a few feet away.

"Mrs. Corbin, I'll be in touch if I have further questions. Please call if you think of anything else," Maor said, handing her a business card.

Maor turned to leave the car, but Candace grabbed her arm.

"Wait! You can't leave me. How do you know that thing won't come back for me?" Candace panicked.

"Mrs. Corbin, we have no reason to believe this creature is targeting you. It appears the target was the councilman. It approached you, yes, but only to scare you, it seems."

Candace nodded with reluctance and her last name struck a chord within Maor again.

"Candace Corbin. Your name is Candace Corbin?" she asked.

"Jesus! This is not the time to make fun of my name, Detective. I get it, comic books. You're not the first to come up with that gem.

Just another reason to hate my husband and his godforsaken name!" Candace snapped, rolling her eyes.

"Is your husband's name *James* Corbin?" Detective Maor asked, ignoring Candace's attitude.

Candace dipped her brow in incredulousness. "Yeah. How did you know that?"

"I've had the pleasure of working with Mr. Corbin on a case recently. He was a consultant, and he's an intelligent man."

Candace grimaced at the detective with disgust. "You know, Detective, that thing, it had James' eyes. At first, I thought it was my imagination. You know, the fear making me see things, but no, those eyes were familiar. They were his; just yellow and filled with evil."

"Detective." A voice called out in the near distance.

Maor turned and saw a tall slender man in full NOPD dress. Three gold stars sat on each shoulder and his dark police hat displayed his polished badge in the center. The brim only slightly covered the scowl on his face.

"Deputy Chief Winslow, I expected you to make the scene tonight. Sir, you won't believe—"

As Detective Maor walked closer to the deputy chief, her eyes widened as she noticed two more city officials behind him.

"Oh... Mayor Johnson and Chief Martel, I wasn't aware that you were here. It appears we have a situation on our hands," she stated; her entire being filled with nerves.

"A *situation*, Detective? One of the city's council members is lying dead on the streets of New Orleans. A city I run. A city you were sworn to protect!" Mayor Johnson barked. "Now we're hearing witnesses confirm the existence of some monster. The news reports are filled with stories of monsters and citizens are already talking with news media. Is this true?"

Mayor Johnson glared at Maor; her hand tapped the side of her leg repeatedly.

I could really use that bottle of vodka in my car right now, Maor thought.

"Yes, ma'am. Every witness, including the significant other of the councilman, stated that it was some sort of beast. Something non-human," Detective Maor answered.

"I'm not buying it. Obviously, we have another serial killer on our hands. A beast? I don't think so. Some deformed lunatic, maybe?" Mayor Johnson finalized.

"We need action on this, Detective. Now with a confirmed

Goliath killer in the media, monster or not, and the daily drug violence, this city is under siege. Where are you on the 'One True God' killer?" Chief Martel inquired in a calm tone that contrasted the mayor's fiery personality.

"I'm making progress, sir," Maor assured. "I may have a suspect, but there is absolutely no evidence to support an arrest. It would help if we could put together a task force for it, and for these Goliath murders. I don't think we can deny this any longer, sir."

"Let me stop you right there, Detective," Chief Martel said. "I'm sure you are aware that we barely have enough patrolmen to answer calls for service, let alone gather enough personnel to supply a task force for these cases! The reason you are the lead detective for both Goliath and 'One True God' is because of your intelligence and ability to get things done. With a city councilman dead, it's time to up your game. Get us a suspect, Detective, and make an arrest. I'm sure the mayor and the hospitality industry would be thankful. Just so you are aware, you'll be hearing about a task force being put together for these cases, probably in the media; it's strictly a public relations move. You are the task force."

Chief Martel's desperate tone made Maor's stomach twist with unease, but the mayor nodded in support of the chief's words. Eager to remove herself from the mayor's company, Detective Maor nodded in agreement, partly insulted that both the chief and mayor expected her to miraculously get a suspect and arrest someone like it was easy.

"Detective!" a patrolman called out, turning Maor's attention away from the mayor and chief. "I have some news from the Fifth Precinct."

Maor sighed with relief and marched over to the patrolman.

"What is it?" she asked.

"Ma'am, it appears that the 5th is working a case similar to the MO of the 'One True God' killer. They're asking if you want to go out and take a look. They said they have a detective on the scene, but he could use the help. They only have two cars for the entire district tonight."

Detective Maor shook her head in disbelief. "Officer, where is Detective Garner?"

"There was a signal 30 in the projects, but that was four hours ago," he replied.

Detective Maor prompted her radio, knowing her co-worker would not be happy about this. "1153 to 1141."

"1141 to 1153," the voice on the other end answered.

"Garner, go to Channel 8."

"What's up, Nola?"

"Garner, I need you here to oversee the processing of the city councilman's scene. There has been another religious murder in the Fifth Precinct and I need to take a look at it. You should know that the brass is out here. City Hall as well."

"Nola, you are uptown. Where is the Second Precinct Investigative Unit?"

"Glorified rookie," she replied.

"Jesus Christ, Nola, you owe me. I'm on my way."

She turned to the officer on scene. "Officer, ensure all witness statements are documented for my review, and all shell casings are collected and logged. Also, see to it that Mrs. Corbin gets home safely after Detective Garner gets here. The coroner is already here to take the body. Just make sure you tow the vehicle and have it impounded. I'll let the Fifth Precinct know that I'm on my way."

Detective Maor turned and waved at the brass, only to receive a few scowls and glares in return, enough motivation for her to leave immediately.

"I need a raise."

CHAPTER
TWENTY-TWO

"One True God."
—Detective Maor

The rotation of police lights illuminated the Lower Ninth Ward neighborhood as dawn drew near. The morning light bled through the windows of Priestess Nadia's Voodoo Emporium.

The front door had been left open, so Detective Maor marched into the makeshift retail store without any effort. Her army boots thumped against the hardwood floor and alerted the two uniformed officers of her presence. The chaos left on the floor was not what she had expected.

"Hey, Serge, the detective from the First Precinct is here," one of the uniformed officers said.

"I can see that, Vic. I'm standing in the same room as you. Do me a favor and make sure there isn't a crowd gathering outside!" the sergeant ordered.

"Sure thing, Sarge," the officer replied, and he left the shop.

"Sergeant Roberts, I'm Detective Nola Maor of the First Precinct. Dispatch told me you had a signal 30 for me to look at?"

"Yeah, I think this one is yours. Victim's name is Nadia Pierre, or Priestess Nadia, as most knew her around these parts. Have a look," the sergeant said in a dismissive tone.

The sergeant directed Maor over to the stiffened body on the floor and Detective Maor rolled her eyes at his indifferent attitude.

"Interesting," she said, refocusing.

Detective Maor inspected the unusual objects that had fallen from the shelves and cluttered the floor. Some of the items such as cups, journals, and handcrafted jewelry were everyday tourist traps, but others looked old and were unfamiliar to her.

In such a small city, Maor remembered the stories about a Voodoo Priestess and her proclivity for spiritual guidance to tourists, but she did not pay it any attention. Most of the people in the city had some sort of hustle. Why would this story be any different?

"Sergeant, was the body found like this?" Maor asked.

"I know what the goddamn job is, Detective. We tried to keep it as it was, but the blood kept flowing over the evidence. You can see why I called you here."

"The victim appears to have a sharp force trauma to the throat. The wound is longer than it is deep so it appears to have been done with a slashing motion by a blade of some sort. Her hands were bound with plastic zip ties, and she is on her left side with her legs bent behind her, which suggests that she kneeled when her throat was cut," Maor said.

"You might want to take a step back, Detective. The blood mostly covered what I'm talking about, but if you look closely, you can still see it," he said.

As Maor stepped around Priestess Nadia, she spotted the blood-colored brush strokes near the victim's head that stretched across the floor. She retrieved a pair of latex gloves from her pocket, and upon closer inspection, she noticed that the brush strokes spelled out the haunting words: 'One True God.'

"Sergeant, I'm not sure this was the 'One True God' killer. Something is off. How did you find out about this?" she asked.

"The neighbor heard two people yelling and a car speed off around 10 p.m. She wasn't sure if the yelling came from inside the residence or not, so it took us a minute to find the body. There were no signs of forced entry, but what you see here of course shows a little bit of a struggle," the sergeant explained.

Detective Maor nodded and analyzed more of the room. The selection of voodoo dolls and trinkets lined up on the shelves gave her goosebumps at the sight of them.

Maor strolled over to the window and noticed the makeshift cash table pressed against the wall beside a wooden walking cane. The craftsmanship of its double-headed snake design impressed her as she held it in her hands, but when she placed the cane back against the wall, she spotted the bound record journal on the table.

"Priestess Nadia was well-liked in the neighborhood. She was a Voodoo practitioner, but more of a spiritual guide for those who visited. She was a powerful woman, but a harmless, gentle soul," the sergeant said in a softer, more compassionate tone.

As Maor listened to the sergeant, she opened the journal to see a list of dates in chronological order with a variety of names written under 'visitors' on each page.

"Well, Sergeant, it looks like the Priestess liked to keep track of the souls who visited her. This book has information on who visited the store, on what date, and the item purchased, if any," Maor explained. "The problem is outside of the painted message, this isn't our killer's MO. The scene is messy, which means he didn't plan as well as before. My guy is meticulous. Plus, there is no gunshot wound; not to mention the victim is female. His victims have all been male so far, so it could be a copycat."

Maor continued to scan the pages and study the names and dates one after the other, but as she read more, one familiar name popped up on a few different dates—James Corbin. Maor's curiosity caused her to skip to the last page in the journal. Her heart raced with anticipation as her eyes wandered to the bottom of the page and stared at the last name scribbled. Deacon Nicholas Bianchi.

"I take back what I said, Sergeant. This is our killer. I believe we have an official suspect; maybe even two."

CHAPTER TWENTY-THREE

"Candy, I'm not through with you yet."
—James Corbin

Candace ambled through The Promenade Mall, window shopping from store to store, and browsing the overpriced merchandise she couldn't afford. Anyone who had experienced such trauma would likely hide away at home, but Candace believed in safety in numbers, so she preferred to venture out for the first time since Goliath murdered Phillip. Her heart ached for him, but nothing could bring him back now.

As she continued through the mall, she overheard some shoppers gossiping about the reports of the beast. Some made jokes, some expressed their fear, and others were still in disbelief. Candace had attempted to escape the isolation of her home to clear her head, so to be reminded of the creature only made her feel more anxious than before. She had replayed the night of Phillip's murder a million times in her mind, trying to process what she had witnessed, but only time would do that. Now, she had therapy shopping to do.

The Fantastic Treat ice cream shop had always been one of Candace's go-to destinations when she visited The Promenade, and when she approached the counter, her tastebuds tingled at the endless ice cream flavors and toppings. A guilty pleasure for every planned and unplanned trip.

A bright smile grew on her face when the sugary smell sparked nostalgic memories of her teenage years, but a sharp twinge in her cheek quickly reminded her of her reality, punishing her for her brief display of joy. The sudden pain made her worry that the beast had scarred her face for good. Candace sighed and refocused on which flavor would console her best.

"Mint chocolate chip," a familiar voice behind her said to the clerk behind the counter. "She likes mint chocolate chip when she's sad."

Candace looked over her right shoulder to see the face that had caused her anger for so long.

"Hello, James. I guess it makes sense for you to be here right now, wouldn't it? Pain from my past showing up while I deal with the pain of today. This time it's the pain in my ass."

James smirked with amusement at her comment and feisty attitude; always one of the traits he loved most about her.

"I know you, Candace. It was only a matter of time before you came here. Just picked the right day, that's all," James said.

"Bullshit. Why are you here? Do you think I'm desperate enough to use you as a rebound or something?" she hissed as she reached for her mint chocolate chip ice cream cone.

"I see I was right about the ice cream," James quipped. "Candace, I only wanted to check on you. I saw everything on the news. I'm sorry you had to experience that; it sounded horrific."

Candace scowled with bitterness, but James gently placed his hand on her shoulder.

Candace stared at James' hand and quickly shunned it away.

"James, I'm not interested in your sympathy. What are you doing here? This isn't a coincidence. You don't like the mall and you definitely don't like to stroll around and window shop. You knew I would be here, and I'm not interested in listening to any pathetic attempt to get me back. What do you want?"

"You're right, Candace. I knew you were here, but I did want to check on your well-being. Although you haven't always been kind to me, I still care for you and want nothing but the best for you," James said. "I didn't know Phillip, but I'm still shaken by his death for you."

"Thank you, James," she said in an icy tone. "Phillip was everything I wanted in a man. He was nothing like you. Your love doesn't matter to me. You were simply a waste of time and I hate you for it. You have caused me nothing but frustration since we've been together. I know why I saw your eyes in that beast when it attacked."

"You know, Candace, you've always known what you wanted, and once upon a time, you wanted me, regardless of what you are saying now," James said, stepping closer to her. "It didn't matter how much I gave you or how hard I worked; it was never good enough for you. You became a vile, mean woman, and an active trigger to my mental and physical pain. When it comes to hate, the feeling is mutual."

"Typical. Always crying about your feelings. Same old James."

"Oh, but Candy, I'm not the 'same old James' anymore. I'm the one giving out the pain now. Just ask your precious Phillip. As for you, Candy, I'm not through with you yet," James threatened with a yellow glow in his eyes.

Candace raised her brow with terror in her eyes as she looked at James. "Those eyes. I saw those eyes two nights ago!"

James scoffed. "What kind of person goes to the mall two days after their lover gets slaughtered? You are the worst person, Candace, and the day you walked out of my life was one of the best days of my life. I'll see you soon. Real soon."

The sweet taste of her ice cream turned sour in Candace's mouth, so she tossed it into the trash and ran out of the mall, upset at the sight of James, and slightly disgusted with herself.

She raced into the parking lot with tears in her eyes and stumbled to her car.

That doesn't make any sense, she thought.

"James is an asshole, but a murderer? He can't be! I saw the beast up close, and it wasn't human," she mumbled.

Candace scanned the parking lot as she trembled in her car.

She had never feared James before, but for some reason, his presence in the mall made her uneasy.

Candace glanced in the rearview mirror and started the engine. She set the air conditioning to full and sighed with relief to be safe.

The cool air rushed upon her face and blew her hair away from her sweaty neck, but the air conditioning offered no relief when she looked in her rearview mirror again and saw James glaring at her from the back seat.

Candace screamed with fright, but James leaned forward and covered her mouth.

"Shhhhhh! Let's not yell. Relax. I just want to talk, Candy," James said.

Candace tried to squeal and wiggle out of James' grip as her labored breathing made her chest tighten. Tears swamped her face as she kicked out in desperation, but her attempt failed against James' strength.

"Candy! Sweet Candy! You ridiculed me. All I wanted to do was be with you. But I wasn't good enough for you, was I?" James taunted, his eyes burning yellow. "You've left me no choice but to hurt you. You gave me pain, so we want your blood in return!"

James started to transform into his beastly state, and Candace squirmed in her seat. She reached out to seize the steering wheel and tried to pull away as she stomped her feet in an attempt to get someone's attention, *anyone's* attention.

James' hand disfigured, and his fingers and nails stretched beyond human capacity as coarse hair grew from his skin. He strengthened his grip and suffocated her as if a plastic bag had been put over her head.

Candace shrieked as best she could, unable to understand what was happening.

"Do you remember me?" the beast growled as its head and shoulders pressed against the roof of Candace's car.

Candace's heart raced with horror as her throat closed up more and more by the second, but as she tried to scream and make herself heard again, Goliath punched her seat and his giant hand pushed through Candace's chest.

Her body weakened and everything went black.

CHAPTER TWENTY-FOUR

"Well, I'm sorry to hear about the councilman."
—James Corbin

The cloudy day provided a refreshing change from the humid summer heat that had melted everyone over the last few months, but Detective Maor couldn't care less. The political squeeze from the NOPD brass was one issue, but not being able to do anything about people losing their lives was another. Her failure had caused a sense of doubt she had not experienced since her childhood, and she had a feeling that her lack of confidence would remain until the two killers on the loose were caught once and for all.

"God, I need a drink," she said.

Maor realized it had been a long time since she evoked His name, but she let the fleeting thought go and refocused on her lead.

She took her eyes off the road momentarily and glanced at Priestess Nadia's ledger on the seat next to her. Two questions repeated in her head, replaying like a terrible song.

How does James know her? Why was he there so frequently?

Maor had her suspicions, but given James' knowledge and love of religion and history, she figured that Nadia's shop appealed to him.

Her foot hit the gas and she soon arrived at James' home.

As she pulled up, the modesty of his house initially surprised her. Although its modest exterior fit his personality when she first met him, she expected something a little more... imposing.

The description of the newly-purchased luxury vehicle in the driveway matched the car registered to the address in the system, and the feminine colors and patterns of the small porch offered a subtle reminder of Candace.

Maor knocked on the glass pane of the front door and listened to its echo inside. As she waited, she noticed that the brand-new ebony door did not quite fit the rest of the house.

"Interesting choice. Must be a replacement," she observed.

Maor knocked again and peered through the textured glass within the door, eventually making her way to the large window, which allowed her to look past the tan curtains and into the living room.

As she stared into the room, a thunderous crash sounded from the rear of the house and made her jump. She darted back to the door and knocked harder, slightly panicked.

"Mr. Corbin! Mr. Corbin, are you there?" Maor yelled.

Maor hurried from the door to the window a few times until she finally spotted James approaching the front door, shirtless and sweating. His chiseled chest and abs were unexpected as his usual clothing gave little away; her heartbeat increased with anticipation as he opened the door.

"Detective, hey. What brings you this way? Not that I'm complaining," James said with an inviting smile.

"James, hello. I'm sorry to disturb you. I'm glad I caught you at home."

"No disturbance at all, Detective. I was just working out. Please, come in," he replied as he stepped aside, allowing her to pass.

The two of them shared an awkward silence as Maor stepped inside, and the absence of James' shirt caused her palms to sweat from nervousness. She slid them back and forth on her pants to hide her clamminess, but her physical attraction to James intensified at the sight of his bare chest.

Maor eyed the firmness of James' chest, and she temporarily forgot why she had visited James, until she noticed the triangular scar in his flesh. A circle sat inside the triangle, and a water droplet hung from the bottom of the circle.

The grotesque scar made Maor tense up, but she couldn't take her eyes away as she tried to identify the unfamiliar symbol.

"M-Mr. Corbin, unfortunately this isn't a social visit. I came here as part of an investigation and I have a few questions for you," she croaked after not speaking for a while.

"Please, call me James," he insisted. "Yes, I saw the news a couple of nights ago. The councilman, right? It's unbelievable. Confirmed sightings by dozens of people of that *thing*. Is it real?"

"Unfortunately, yes, it's real. We are dealing with something I initially thought to be a fairytale," Maor confirmed.

"Well, it is New Orleans, Detective. Home to all kinds of weird happenings. I'm sorry to hear about the councilman. Why would it target him or was it some sort of coincidence?" James asked.

Maor watched James grab the T-shirt on the recliner and threw it on to cover himself, clearing her throat with disappointment.

"We are still investigating the details. Tell me, Mr. Corbin, do you know who the councilman was dating?" Maor questioned.

James shook his head and furrowed his brow. "No, I didn't know the councilman. Why would I know who he dated?"

"Candace Corbin, your wife," she said.

Maor eyed James for a reaction, *any* reaction.

Deep down, she hoped he would display shock or hurt, as she had always preferred a man who openly expressed his emotions.

"She was with him when Goliath attacked," she said.

James' face remained blank. "My wife and I have split. Neither of us have any interest in resolution."

James turned away from Maor and gazed out the window as he had so many times before.

"Christ, James, even though you two have split, aren't you a little bit worried about her well-being? Have you talked to her?" Maor asked, incredulous.

"I haven't," he answered.

"Well, apparently the beast got up close and personal with her, which put quite a scare in her. For some reason, it only put a scar on her face and didn't want her dead."

James nodded. "Well, I'm glad she's okay."

"Yes, but she said something strange, James. She said Goliath had your eyes. Obviously, you're human, but how bad did your marriage get that your wife sees you in a monster?"

James stood and smiled at Maor's subtle accusation.

"I don't appreciate the accusation, Detective. No matter how subtle. She is the monster, not me. When we got married, she was one of the sweetest people I had ever met. These days she is cold and cruel to me. Forgive me if I don't care about how she feels," he defended; his skin heated at the thought of Candace. "If you don't need me for a consult, Detective, I'd like to get back to my workout."

"Actually, James, we're just getting started," Maor said, her face tensing.

Her instincts sharpened, and for the first time since she met James, she saw him as a suspect. His lack of empathy for Candace showed a darker side to the man she had a slight infatuation for and admired.

"What now, Detective? Again, is there something you need my consult on?" he snapped.

"Are you familiar with a woman by the name of Nadia Pierre, aka Priestess Nadia?" she asked.

"Of course, she's a great friend who I've known for years. I love what she does for people, and she can talk religious academics as well as any stuffed shirt at a conference I would attend," James explained with a cheery tone. "Why do you ask? Am I being replaced by her? If so, I would completely understand. She's very capable."

Maor raised her eyebrows in surprise, as James' tone gave her an idea exactly what his relationship with Nadia was.

"James, she was murdered last night," Maor stated.

James knitted his brow and squinted. "That's impossible. I visited her last night and she was fine. We talked for a while, and I left quite late." James collapsed in a nearby chair; his voice cracked and his eyes welled.

"Yes, I know you were there, James. You know I don't discuss the particulars of a case, but the deaths that have taken place have put me in a desperate position," Maor said, and she pulled Nadia's journal from her bag. "James, Priestess Nadia kept a ledger that recorded every person who visited her shop, displayed interest in an item, and purchased an item. Your name is in there several times, including the night she died."

Maor allowed James to flick through and read his name throughout the book, and he also noticed a familiar name below his own.

"Hell yes, my name should be in there several times! Nadia was a *friend!* She helped me during my dark days and when I needed guidance. How? When?"

James stood and paced the room as fresh tears trickled down his face.

"Dark days?" Maor queried.

James sighed "Yes, I suffered with severe depression and anxiety. I used to be ashamed to admit it, but Nadia helped me."

"There is no shame in that, James," Maor said. "You said

suffered, so I'm glad you got the help you needed."

"I didn't get any help. I conquered it myself. Psychiatrists are for the weak."

Maor scoffed. "Bullshit. You are too smart to say something so ignorant."

"Whatever," James snapped. "Can you please tell me how and when she died?"

Maor stared at James, sympathetic to his plea for answers.

"Shit, this goes against my better judgment, so we'll play this like a consultation, James. But I need you to be honest with me and give me as much information as you can!"

"Fine."

"Was Priestess Nadia into anything illegal?" Maor asked.

"No, of course not. She was a spiritual guide. Her only interest was helping others. Everyone loved her," James answered, disbelieving that anyone could ask such a thing about her.

Maor nodded and scribbled some notes into a small black notepad. "The shop—she sold those items as religious trinkets, yes? Was she trying to convert others?"

"No. She believed everyone had their own path. She used her religion to help others find it. The items she sold...well, that's a different story," James said with a smile. "Tell me, Nola—can I call you Nola?"

"Yes," she answered. Her heart pounded hearing her name pass James' lips for the first time.

"Nola, do you believe in the supernatural?"

Maor exhaled with amusement. "Before the other night, no, but with that thing running around killing people, how can I not?"

"Well, the items in that shop have an energy to them, and they become attracted to certain people. Some of the items can be dangerous."

Maor frowned. "What do you mean, dangerous?"

"Nadia told me that it depends on the type of person you are. The trinkets don't judge character; it's an energy match. She said that if the person found their suited trinket, it would help them find a path. Nadia even claimed some objects would manifest themselves in her shop from the other side to connect with a soul."

Maor stared at James in disbelief, but he spoke as though he believed every word of it.

"So... it wasn't all about religion?" she followed up.

"Religion? Not always. I guess some would come for religious answers; a subject near and dear to my own heart. Faith, if you have it, can have an incredible impact on your life."

"It can have an impact all right," she scoffed, rolling her eyes. "Enough with the fairy tales, James. Did you get any of these trinkets for yourself last night?"

"Fairy tales, Nola? Don't tell me you're a cliché. High intelligence means you don't believe in religion or the occult?"

"Religion has failed me, James, like so many others. That's my cliché. That, and I'm another cop who likes to drink. What I will say is that even though the supernatural world seems to be real, religion is still causing people to die. Again, your name is in the book for that night. Is it because you went to get an item?"

"Before I answer your question, let me tell you that religion has not failed you. There are many practicing religions, but they all mostly originated from a single concept of darkness and light. This concept brings us all on different paths, but these paths cross—"

"Thank you for the religious advocacy speech, James. It's noted, but let me stop you right there. Let's stick to the topic at hand. Since you were only there that night to see a friend, is there anything you can tell me that might help? Her murder didn't fit the suspect's typical MO, but I think she became another victim of the 'One True God' killer. Did you notice anything different about that night?" Maor asked.

"Wait, yes...I did see someone else that night. A white guy, I think. He drove up as I left. I thought he was some sort of tourist. Damn it! Why didn't I stay with her longer?" James said, sitting back down, weakened from the thought.

Maor's heart rate increased at James' vague description; the odds of another random tourist so close to the Priestess' time of death was slim.

"I knew it!" Maor exclaimed. "James, I have to leave, but I'll be in touch. Thank you for your help. I'm sorry for the loss of your friend."

Maor got up and walked toward the door, but James paced behind her. "Wait! You said it didn't fit his MO; what was different?" he asked.

Maor hesitated, but she concluded that the information wasn't enough to hinder the investigation.

"He slit her throat," she revealed, and she turned back to the door. "Goodbye, James."

DESCENT OF A BROKEN MAN

James remained calm after hearing the details of Nadia's murder, but his composure was short-lived.

I'm sorry Nadia. I let my need to torture Candace distract me. I should have been there for you. I let you down.

His mind focused on one word, a word that had passed his lips with bloody intentions and had been written under his name in Nadia's ledger that night.

Bianchi.

CHAPTER
TWENTY-FIVE

"Mr. Corbin, why are you here?"
—Dr. Wilson

Dr. Wilson walked the empty halls of Robert E. Lee hours after the dismissal bell had rung. The deafening quiet of the hallways amplified the rhythmic tapping of her heels as she made her way from door to door of each classroom peering inside.

If I could have it this quiet when the students were here, then my job would be accomplished, she thought.

"Dr. Wilson," an older man yelled from across the hall.

Dr. Wilson's head quickly turned in his direction, as she clasped her blouse. "Jesus Christ, Danny, you scared me! Are you finished cleaning for the evening?"

"Yes, ma'am. I'm all done. I was about to leave for the evening, but I was looking for you because you have an old face here to see you," Danny said as he waved the visitor over.

"Hello, Dr. Wilson. It's good to see you again," James said, grinning.

"Mr. Corbin? What on earth are you doing here?"

"I decided to pass by because I wanted to talk to you about some things. Something very important," James responded.

Dr. Wilson's lips pursed and her fist clinched as she exhaled deeply at the sight of the grin on James' face.

"Have a good evening, Danny. Mr. Corbin, please, step into my office. I believe you already know where it is," Dr. Wilson said. Her lips once again pursed.

"I never thought I would be inside these walls again, or even sitting in this damn chair again across from you."

"I was hoping never to see you again as well. I have heard about your progress in life. I have to say that I'm rather surprised. I didn't think you had it in you," Dr. Wilson said.

"You knew damn well I did. You stole my program for Christ's sake. You don't steal anything unless you see value in it," I replied.

Dr. Wilson opened her briefcase and began to add files inside, no longer looking in his direction.

"Mr. Corbin, why are you here? Get to the point of your visit because I'm leaving for the day."

"I know there are some programs the school is affiliated with through the school board and the community that help with students' after school activities. Are you familiar with someone by the name of Bianchi? I've heard he was involved in the community. Only, not many people will give me details about him."

"I'm familiar with the name and the organization he is a part of. He has helped a couple of our troubled junior high kids. His name is Deacon Nicholas Bianchi. He's with St. Mark's Catholic Church and the S.H.A.P.E organization. I've never met him personally, but I've heard a lot of good things about him. What would someone like you want with him?" Dr. Wilson asked.

"More research. I'd like to talk to him about what he's done in the city. I see you are still the same miserable person you've always been. I don't want to be here longer than I need to be."

Dr. Wilson picked up her briefcase and walked toward her office door; her eyes fixed on the floor.

"If there isn't anything else, Mr. Corbin, I'd like to leave before it gets too dark."

"It's Professor Corbin now, Wilson. You should definitely get home soon. The violence in this city is out of control. I heard about what happened to Damon and Cynthia. I would hate to see anything happen to you. Have a good evening, Dr. Wilson."

As James left her office, the phone rang and Dr. Wilson rolled her eyes in frustration. She darted over to answer as she watched James hurry down the hallway.

"Robert E. Lee High School, this is Principal Wilson speaking." Dr. Wilson continued to look out of the windows of the administrative office until James was no longer in sight. She listened to the voice on the other end of the line. "Honey, I'm leaving now. I had an unexpected visitor I had to meet with, which set me behind a little. See you soon."

DESCENT OF A BROKEN MAN

A crashing metallic sound came from the hallway as Dr. Wilson hung up the phone. Her hands shook, as she rushed to the window and peered out into the hallway. Dr. Wilson slowly walked toward the door, crept out into the hall, and scanned the area.

"Danny? Is that you?" she shouted down the hallway of the quiet and dimly lit school. Her hands grabbed at the side of her pants to wipe away the moisture. "James?" she continued to yell as she slowly stepped down the hall.

After she turned the corner, the sight of shredded and twisted metal student lockers caused her eyes to widen. Dr. Wilson's steps were shaky as her legs quivered.

"How...what?" she mumbled, confused at what she saw. The subtle sound of a growling animal nearby sent chills down her spine as she turned to investigate. Dr. Wilson's eyes welled as she whimpered at the glimpse of the beastly figure that stood at the other end of the hall.

"Get out of my school," she demanded,; her voice trembled. She timidly took several steps back.

The subtle yellow glow of its eyes intensified as the beast released another more intense growl. Dr. Wilson found the strength to move her legs as she turned and ran. The sound of the beast's claws scratched against the tile as it gave chase. Her legs were unable to move with the same vigor as when she was younger. Dr. Wilson slipped and fell to the hard tile as she turned the corner in the hall. Her knees and elbows pushed against the floor as she crawled in panic at the sound of the predator behind her.

Dr. Wilson screamed as she felt the pressure of the creature's claws grab her by the back of the neck and lift her off the ground. Her feet kicked as she struggled to find the ground; the pain of her body weight pulled at her frail neck. The sound of the beast's laughter terrified her as it tossed her down the hallway. Her body thumped against the floor, sliding a few extra feet. Blood poured from her mouth as she exhaled and continued to try and push away on her back. Dr. Wilson watched as the beast stomped toward her.

"Why? W-what have I ever done to you?" she pleaded.

The beast walked closer and stood over her, bending over as its teeth neared her face. Tears fell from Dr. Wilson's eyes as she felt the beast's heated breath upon her face.

"Pathetic little woman," it replied to her as it placed its claw on her chest and pinned her to the floor.

The words from the beast struck her memory. Her tears stopped and her eyes once again widened as she remembered the words once told to her by James.

"I know who—"

The beast slowly applied pressure to her chest. Dr. Wilson felt her ribs crack as the claw of the beast pushed through. Blood poured from her mouth and chest as the life in her eyes extinguished.

CHAPTER TWENTY-SIX

"My Lord, you have sent me to a place where my work is plentiful." —Deacon Bianchi

"Good afternoon, I'm Donald Neilson. The brutal murders that have plagued New Orleans and the surrounding areas have gained federal attention as the FBI has contacted city and state officials to form a joint task force to help supplement the scarce financial and manpower resources of the New Orleans Police Department. There were six more drug-related shootings overnight, all without suspects. In addition, the murder of a well-known community Voodoo priestess, which occurred two nights ago, appears to be another victim of the so called 'One True God' serial killer.

City officials continue to discredit the eyewitness reports of a vicious beast murdering more than a dozen people, and further eyewitnesses continue to come forward to speak with the media about what they saw the night City Councilman Phillip Lester was murdered. The citizens of New Orleans have not been scared to come out of their homes, but the local tourist industry has taken a significant dip since the city's murder rate reached national attention. The mayor has refused to expand on the city's plan, but only stated that the federal help is a welcome addition to the team. The New Orleans Police Chief issued a statement saying all investigations are still ongoing, and if you have any information regarding any of the murders in the 'One True God' or so-called 'Goliath' cases, please call the toll-free tip hotline 1-888-556-TIPS."

Deacon Bianchi sat in the community office he once shared with Reverend Jackson at S.H.A.P.E. headquarters and smiled as he watched the 12 p.m. news. Although, his usually pale face was even more flush at the lack of gratefulness the media had shown for the obvious repercussions of those idolators. His satisfaction with the punishment of those sinners was tempered. The events of the past couple of days gave Bianchi a new purpose with the validated existence of Goliath in the flesh by the many witnesses reported at the politician's murder scene.

"My Lord, you have sent me to a place where my work is plentiful. The fornication, the murder, the worshiping of false gods, and now, even the devil in the flesh. You have passed judgment, and this city needs to be brought to its knees. Thank you, Lord, for bringing me here. This city doesn't deserve your mercy," Bianchi said with elation. His thoughts revisited what he had done a few nights ago.

The punishment of Priestess Nadia had been one of Bianchi's most satisfying judgments. Her ability to reach so many people, peddling influence, and the worship of dark magic, idols, and false gods, made her one of the most egregious offenders he had ever encountered.

"We definitely picked the right city to build this program in, Reverend. With the murder of a political figure and the gang violence, it comes as no surprise that the devil manifested here, but it doesn't matter. The Lord will not abandon you, New Orleans. Isn't that right, Reverend?" Bianchi said to the memorial picture of Reverend Jackson, which hung nearby on the wall, as he kissed the rosary in his hand. "I do wish I could have convinced you to stay on the proper path, old friend."

Bianchi refocused after he reflected on his late friend and tempered his own enthusiasm for divine judgment. He tucked his light blue button-down shirt into his slacks when something dawned on him.

"There were headlights when I arrived at the Priestess's house that night, so someone must have seen my car or possibly me. If I'm going to hunt this beast, I need to know what NOPD knows, especially before the federal government comes to their rescue. I can't think of a better way than eliminating that flippant detective leading the investigation."

Bianchi thought about the details of the detective as he slowly paced the room, and the talking heads from the newscast in the background became background noise.

DESCENT OF A BROKEN MAN

"The detective obviously has her suspicions about me, and rightfully so, but unfortunately for her, she is too smart for her own good. She has turned her back on you, Lord, and her lack of faith deserves your judgment as well. I shall pay her a visit."

CHAPTER
TWENTY-SEVEN

"Like you? I'm nothing like you!"
—Detective Maor

The cooler weather made life more bearable for the people in the city.

Detective Maor noticed that barbecues and block parties had popped up everywhere on her way back to the First Precinct Police Station, but she also observed many kids playing outside. They wouldn't have caused her much alarm if they were kicking a ball around or doing handstands, but they all ran after each other with their arms raised in the air and their hands crunched in the shape of claws, growling like the beast. Maor knew that Phillip Lester's murder was national news, but she didn't expect the kids to know so much about the monster. Most likely the resulted outcome of adults who talked about the gruesome details in the presence of children.

As she pulled into the station's car port, she passed a few of her coworkers who conversed before the start of their shift. Maor doubted that their conversation mirrored everyone else's discussions in the city, but the beast was real, regardless of how the city officials tried to spin it.

Maor parked and took a deep breath to gather herself after another long night.

The casual interview of James capped off an interesting afternoon. While her fellow officers were enamored with the gossip of the supernatural, Maor could not shake the regret of what happened to Priestess Nadia. The angst in dealing with the existence of this beast only made her thirsty for the bottle under her car seat. *If this thing is real, what else is out there? Vampires? Werewolves? Fucking Santa Claus?* she thought.

Maor waved and smiled at everyone gathered under the large concrete carport, and she received a few expressions that varied from worried to envy, so she tried her best to dismiss their concerns and refocus on the task at hand.

"Why is James connected to the two high-profile murders?" Maor pondered. "Not only connected but he had a personal relationship with a victim *and* a witness. Could it be that he and Priestess Nadia were just friends? And what is that horrific symbol scarred into his chest?"

Maor grabbed her notepad and sketched the symbol inside.

"James said he visited Nadia often because they were good friends, and she was also a spiritual counselor to many. A Voodoo queen with spiritual guidance and an occult paraphernalia store? She may as well have had a target painted on her back for Bianchi," she continued. "But what brought Bianchi to the lower Ninth Ward? His name is in that book... twice. What was their first encounter like?"

Maor leaned back in her seat and stared out the window, as she contemplated the pieces to the puzzle.

"Hmm, Nadia's reputation might have been enough to land on Bianchi's radar," Maor suggested. "James, I don't know if you're involved with Bianchi or if you have some of the worst luck known to man, but I'll find out. First, though, I need to get this psycho off the streets!"

The room erupted with laughter as three other detectives sat in the corner of the office and continued their daily ritual of sports talk and sexual conquest, an unwelcome distraction.

Maor rolled her eyes at the boy's club when her phone sounded; the ringing cut through the noise in the room.

The sound jolted her, but she answered before it had the opportunity to ring again.

"First Precinct Police Station, this is Detective Maor," she said.

"Hello, Detective," a voice with an Italian accent replied. "It's been a while since we last spoke. I assume you have been looking for me?"

"Hello, David. It has been a while since we have spoken. What makes you think I'm interested in looking for you?" Detective Maor replied in a passive tone, hoping to get a rise out of him.

"Come now, Detective, you believe me to be a murderer. The fact that you parked outside my home and watched me would have been a waste of time if you did not," he said obnoxiously. "And... considering you called me 'David,' that lets me know you have done your homework."

"I know exactly who you are, Bianchi. I also know exactly *what* you are," Maor snapped. "I know you are responsible for the deaths of all those innocent people in my city. You're a psycho, all in the name of a fictitious God and a flawed religion! Your God won't save you. I will find the hard evidence I need to put you in fucking jail!"

The merriment in the room fell silent as her colleagues listened, and Bianchi continued to guffaw on the other end of the phone.

"Your insults have no bearing, but the disrespect toward God will have a price, Detective. Besides, I've done my homework as well. You grew up as a good Catholic girl, didn't you? But you let the actions of one demon in disguise catapult the destruction of your faith?" Bianchi challenged. "God tested you that day and you failed. You are weak, Nola."

Maor's stomach twisted with discomfort at the sound of Bianchi using her first name.

"Obviously, Father Williams was not the only demon who has disguised himself in holy garb. It seems to happen quite often. You are just the latest. What kind of God lets that happen? The harming of innocents by those who are supposed to be leaders of the church. A non-existent one, that's who! If there is a God, he'll help me strap you to a chair," Detective Maor barked with rage as her colleagues observed.

"Detective, have you considered that maybe you are looking at this all wrong? Throughout your decorated law enforcement career, you have always been in a position to stop these monsters. Even with that incident in your past, you were put in a position that saved that young girl's life. There *is* a God, Detective, and like me, maybe you are one of his soldiers. He chose you to carry that burden because he knows you can. Besides, I didn't call you to antagonize you, but to inform you. The devil himself is on the loose in this city, and if you back off, I will put an end to it."

"Like you? I'm nothing like you! You're a monster. I don't need your help. I have what I need to bring you in for questioning. Do me a favor; when I see you, please resist," she yelled, standing to her feet.

"Have it your way, Detective. You will see me soon, but in the meantime, have another drink. I'm sure that bottle of vodka under your car seat is quite lonely," Bianchi shouted over the noise in the background, and he abruptly ended the call.

Detective Maor pulled the receiver from her ear and stared at it; her ears ringing from the noise on the other end.

The sound of a boat horn and a popcorn vender yelling gave her Bianchi's exact location.

"The Riverwalk," she said, marching to the door.

"Hey, Maor! You're needed on a scene in Jefferson Parish!" her sergeant informed her from across the room.

"Excuse me? I don't work for JP. I'm on my way to do something," she replied.

"You'll want to go to this one. That fuckin' monster killed again, and this time, it's your witness from the councilman's murder. Umm... Corbin is the name."

Maor tilted her head. "Candace Corbin?"

"Yeah, that's it," the sergeant answered.

"What the hell? Fine, I'm on my way," Maor said, and she stormed out of the office, slamming the door behind her.

CHAPTER
TWENTY-EIGHT

"New Orleans deserves better than this."
—Detective Maor

━━━━━━━━━━━━━━━━━━━━━━━━━━━━━━━━━━━━━━

"Sergeant, I'm Detective Nola Maor of NOPD's First Precinct. You requested the lead detective on the Goliath cases?" she inquired.

Maor and the sergeant stood in the center of the Promenade Mall parking lot and stared at Candace's luxury vehicle. One of the rear side doors had been twisted and broken off, and dark blood covered the beige interior.

Maor instantly recognized Candace and covered her mouth at the sight of the gaping hole in her chest with her bloodless face and lifeless eyes.

"Thank you for calling me, Sergeant. That's definitely my witness," Maor confirmed. "Judging by the damage to the rear door and the other cars nearby, I suppose you have the same suspect in mind."

The sergeant broke out into a deep belly laugh, and Maor frowned at the joke she had clearly missed. In fact, she felt a little insulted by his unprofessionalism, causing her to shake her head in annoyance and sneer as she tried to work out what had amused him.

"Forgive me, Detective," the sergeant apologized, clearing his throat and recomposing himself. "I've been on the job for eighteen years now and never thought I would receive witness statements that point toward monsters and beasts. It's surreal. Anyway... yes, several witnesses have reported seeing Goliath flee the scene. We found your card in the vehicle, so we thought our victim might be part of your investigation."

"I appreciate the professionalism, Sergeant. Forward me the report, if you don't mind," Detective Maor said, anxious to get back to her part of the city.

"Good luck hunting that thing, Detective. Seeing what it did here, it needs to be put down," the sergeant said. "Oh, and do you know if the victim has any relatives we can notify?"

James flickered through Maor's mind; the closest person to Candace, but also a reoccurring factor in her investigation.

"Yes, I know of one. I'll advise him."

As Maor drove back to Orleans Parish, the gravity of Candace's murder weighed on her, and the events of the past few days played back in her mind.

"An assassination of a city councilman, the murder of a witness, *and* the murder of a citizen all have a connection to James in one way or another. The question is: why so many in his circle? This is more than a coincidence. I need to pay Mr. Corbin another visit, and there is no time like the present," Maor said, working through her thoughts aloud as if someone sat beside her.

As her drive continued, the intrusive ring from the passenger side seat caused her to quickly pick up the cell phone as she sighed. She smiled as she glanced at the small screen when she identified the number of the incoming call.

"Where have you been? I know you watch the news, lady." Maor smiled as she answered.

"I've been right here watching with a close eye. I know how you get when you have a case that gets a little rough. I wanted to make sure you didn't have any distractions, little sis. How are you holding up?" Janice asked.

"It's fucking crazy down here, Janice. Another religious psycho and a real live monster. The church, momma, and daddy, no one told us this stuff was real. I feel like I'm losing my mind trying to wrap my head around it all."

"If you only knew what was really out there," Janice answered.

"Wait. What?"

"There are things I can't talk about, sis, but a lot of the stuff we thought was fairy tales are real and dangerous."

"Janice, what are you talking about? What things?"

"Look, I wanted to check on you and give you a heads up that Quantico is sending a team down there. The Mayor and the Chief of Police asked for help and from what I've heard, they are desperate. I would have come myself, but since I'm so far along in my pregnancy, both my husband and the bosses don't want me down there."

Detective Maor fell silent as she listened to Janice. Her lips pursed at the thought of an FBI team coming here and taking over her investigations.

"No, you don't need to be down here, Janice. Not with Goliath running around. I don't know what it is or how to stop it. Reports claim it withstood gunfire and it didn't slow it down. I need you and my niece or nephew to be safe. An FBI badge won't protect you if we come face-to-face with that thing."

"Uh... reminder, I'm the big sister here. Just remember whatever you need to do to get your cases wrapped up, you only have a day or two before FBI agents will have their hands in everything. Find out how to stop those two sons-of-bitches and put them down... permanently, if you have to," Janice said, her voice slightly higher.

Her thoughts bounced back and forth between the two killers, much like a tennis ball during a match, but the thought of telling the brass that a witness had been murdered would probably guarantee the end of her career.

"I just had a witness killed, so I'm sure my time with the department is on shaky ground. Before they try to take my badge, I will finish this. One True God and Goliath have spilled so much blood in this city that not even neighborhood dope dealers are risking being on the street at night," Maor continued. "The news broadcast has speculated the motivations of both killers for months now, pushing fear into the community, but New Orleans deserves better than this."

"Get it done. You're a Maor. It's what we do. I love you," Janice firmly stated.

"I'm on it, sis. I love you too," Maor replied as she hung up her phone.

Detective Maor wiped the only tear that rolled down her cheek away as her radio prompted.

"306 to 1153."

"1153 to 306."

"Detective, can you go to channel three?"

"Okay, 306, I'm here," Maor advised.

"Detective, we have a brutal signal 30 over here at Robert E. Lee High School. It looks like that monster made its way inside the school. It killed one of the faculty members. Victim's name is Dr. Edna Wilson. She is... she was the principal."

"Wait! Did you say Dr. Edna Wilson? The principal?"

"Um... that's exactly what I said. Evidence is telling me and my partner it was that beast. It destroyed some lockers and crushed her sternum. I mean, pushed a hole right through it," the officer said.

Maor's hands trembled when the officer relayed the information. As she heard the name of the victim, the weight of the radio felt as if it was twice as heavy as before. Maor tried to lift the radio to respond, but detailed images of every crime scene from Goliath's victims flooded her memories.

"Thank you, Officer. Secure the scene. Get the rank and crime lab out there and get it all processed. I'm on my way to follow up on another case right now. I'll be there shortly," Detective Maor said somberly.

"10-4, Detective. I'll advise the Sergeant."

One more body connected to you, James. What the fuck is going on?

During the short drive, Maor replayed her last conversation with James in her head, and some red flags concerned her.

Firstly, the strange symbol on his chest.

Secondly, the lack of concern for someone he once loved.

And thirdly, at some point in the conversation, his body language revealed a man eager to get out of her presence.

He couldn't wait to get rid of me, she thought.

Maor parked on the adjacent street corner of James' home, so she could scope out his residence and keep her vehicle out of his view.

As she left her car and crossed the street, she saw that James' car was missing from the driveway, but when she walked closer, she noticed that James had left the living room light on, suggesting his presence.

But when she peeked inside, she did not see any movement.

Maor decided that he had probably stepped out, but then remembered that he seemed to like working out at the back of the house. With this in mind, Maor crept through the alleyway next to his house, peering through each window on the way.

When she reached the rear of the house, she remembered the loud crashing noise that sounded on her last visit. James said it was the weights from his workout, but Maor did not believe him.

She scanned the back yard to see if anything appeared out of place, but nothing stood out, except the well-kept lawn and the back door's splintered frame. Only a portion of it was still attached to its hinges, and the deadbolt had been broken into pieces. Shards of the frame were scattered on the linoleum floor near James' washing machine, and the damage prompted Maor to squeeze the button on her radio.

"1153."

"1153, go 'head," the voice on the other end replied.

Maor's training pushed her to call for backup, but her instincts told her that maybe some time alone in James' house would reveal a thing or two about what he had been hiding.

"1153 to dispatch, disregard, ma'am," Maor answered after a brief pause.

"10-4," the dispatcher acknowledged.

"Hello, New Orleans Police," she yelled as she set foot inside the house; her voice echoed throughout the house.

Maor drew her weapon and edged through the spacious home. The rooms were all well-kept, and the neat, feminine decor made her question whether James had any say in the furnishings. Maor recalled Candace's strong personality and assumed that James gave her carte blanche to decorate the house as she wanted.

As Maor moved around the house, she pointed her gun downward with her arms bent at the elbows and pressed against her chest. She peered around the entrance of a hallway and pressed her back against the adjacent wall.

Maor always laughed at the officers in the movies who held their guns near their heads. One stumble and that officer could have an embarrassing accidental death.

Maor spotted a lone door in the hallway and shuffled toward it with extended arms, ready to fire if needed. She pushed the door open and entered a dimly-lit room that contained a desk and some wooden bookshelves.

James' personal office perhaps, Maor thought.

The computer that sat on the desk looked to be dusted regularly, and the array of books on the shelves were in alphabetical order and undisturbed.

"I'm not sure what happened to the door, but no burglary has occurred here. Nothing is out of place or unusual," Maor concluded, lowering her gun.

ASHON RUFFINS

Maor's initial unease dissipated as she stood in James' office for a little longer, clearly alone in the house, but her heart plummeted when she looked down at the floor. A large symbol had been painted on the wood in front of the desk, the same symbol she saw on James' chest.

Maor had no idea what the symbol meant, but her instincts told her it was more than a coincidence that the symbol carved onto his chest was painted on the floor. Then, she noticed that the painting had been covered with dried blood.

Maor stared at the symbol and descended into deep thought. "Hmm. There's no spatter or spray, and there aren't any repairs or new furniture either. If a struggle happened here, it occurred quickly, but... nothing in this house points toward a fight."

Maor surveyed the room in more detail, but she still didn't find anything unusual.

Books on history and religion, stacks of papers and magazines, but nothing else out of the ordinary. The room had been painted with practical earth tones, and James' desk had been left neat and tidy as if there were a place for everything.

Upon Maor's inspection, she spotted an expensive-looking letter opener on the desk with a gold and white handle —and red spots splattered on the silver blade.

"More blood," she whispered as she read the carving on the handle: *'Your journey will be powerful, Love, Dad'*. Maor hurriedly pulled her cell phone from her back pocket, flipped it open, and took a photo of the letter opener.

As Maor's heart raced, she turned her attention to the leather book on the desk, slightly hidden by several sheets of paper. The cover had no title, only two symbols—one of which had been painted on the floor and seared into James' chest.

Maor's hands trembled with fright, but she grabbed the book and opened its pages.

A surge of energy radiated from the book, and the symbol Maor had come to recognize glowed white, but as soon as Maor registered what happened, the light dimmed.

Dazed, Maor jumped at the sound of a car door slamming outside, and she hurried from the office back to the living room.

As she peered through the living room window, she saw James climbing the stairs, returning home.

"Oh shit!" Maor whispered, and she sprinted to the back of the house with the book in hand, trying not to make a sound.

She slipped through the back door and darted through the alleyway, stooping to avoid being seen from a window.

Once Maor made it to the front yard undetected, she peered into the front window and watched James stroll to the back of the house.

Maor sighed with relief and rushed back to her car on the corner. She threw the strange book onto the passenger seat and reversed down the street as fast as she could.

Inside, James ambled through his home, still distracted by the pleasurable encounters with his wife and with Dr. Wilson. The fear in both of their eyes as he killed them filled him with glee and forced an uncontrollable grin onto his face, but his elation didn't last as long as he had hoped.

"What?!" James exclaimed, halting outside his office.

James *knew* he didn't keep his office door open or leave the light on when he went out.

He charged inside, panicked, and scanned the room, discovering that the *Book of Blood* had gone missing.

A gut-wrenching pain in the pit of James' stomach made him groan and wince, but that pain soon turned to anger at the sight of the empty space on his desk.

"Who the fuck knows?" he growled, his breathing erratic.

James' pupils glowed yellow, and his teeth grew once again. The beast within him roared with rage, but after a few agonizing minutes, the room fell silent.

CHAPTER TWENTY-NINE

"I'll see you soon."
—James Corbin

Since I became a member of the faculty, I found that the university overcompensated with the air conditioning in the classrooms during the summer. I didn't object to it. The essence of Ahriman often ran warm within me.

At the beginning, I cherished the power Ahriman gave me, but his essence caused a constant burning thirst and desire within me to spill blood. So, I often ended my lectures early to soothe my dry mouth and adjust my often-uncomfortable clothes. The students didn't care, and it also gave me an extra ten minutes to work out how to find Bianchi and my stolen book.

As I rushed across campus, a flyer stapled to the information board in the student union caught my attention. The heading on the flyer read:

S.H.A.P.E. Community Social and Youth Gathering.

Perfect, I thought, making a mental note of the time and place.

My professorship should help me blend in and reach a couple of kids who could point me in the right direction. *Bianchi may be a murderous psychopath, but I can't deny that S.H.A.P.E. has had a positive influence on the youth in the city. I don't care. It won't save him. He killed my friend, and for that, blood shall be spilled.*

S.H.A.P.E used a converted school satellite building as their headquarters, which had plenty of paved parking out front, and wired fencing. A perfect location to contain the festivities and create a sense of security in a crime-ridden neighborhood.

The small crowd on the paved parking lot outside the building worried me a bit, but I tried to convince myself that there were still enough people who could potentially give me the cover I needed and the information I desired.

After I scouted the people and their behavior for a while, I strolled through the gates of the community festival and blended into the crowd around me.

Even with less attendees than I had expected, children of all ages played with footballs and shot hoops on the pavement in the far corner, and food vendors had tables of finger food set up along the fence lines.

A DJ performed clean versions of adult-oriented music, and a few of the parents danced to the beat, while they congregated with each other and enjoyed the party atmosphere.

The presence of school board officials, politicians, medical professionals, and even law enforcement, impressed me and suggested that S.H.A.P.E. was the real deal; an organization that could get things done within the troubled city.

I hope so. They'll just have to do it without Bianchi, I thought to myself.

The community leaders and officers spoke with a few troubled youths, likely drug dealers, which surprised me even more. I hated interacting with troublesome teens as a teacher, so the sight of them filled me with resentment as I ambled through the festival. The past couple of days I found it hard to interact with anyone on a social level.

The bass from the speakers reverberated in my chest, but my attention focused on a middle-aged, African-American pastor who stood at the entrance to the S.H.A.P.E facility, laughing with two teenage boys.

Sweat covered his face as he stood in a thick maroon suit, but the handkerchief he kept using to dab his forehead did little to help.

I again shifted in my clothes, unable to get comfortable in my own skin. Regardless, I was filled with amusement and approached him with a welcoming smile. "How ya doin,' Pastor?"

"I'm doing well this evening, sir," the pastor replied, and he turned back to the teenage boys. "Excuse me for a moment, kids." The boys nodded and rushed over to the buffet tables, and the pastor spun back to face me.

"I'm sorry. I don't believe we've met?"

"No, we haven't. My name is James Corbin. I'm a professor over at the university uptown. I've heard about all the good you have been doing in the community, so I had to come and see for myself. I wanted to see if I could be of any use to you and the organization, Pastor Bianchi," I said, trying to coerce information from him by calling him by the wrong name.

"Not a man of faith, are you, Mr. Corbin?" the pastor assumed, a hint of frustration in his sarcastic tone. "My name is Pastor Kevin Lockwell and I'm a Baptist minister at New Hope Baptist Church here in the city. Deacon Bianchi is my Catholic partner for this establishment, Deacon Nicholas Bianchi of St. Mark's. He's around here somewhere, I'm sure. He's a little socially awkward, but he's done a lot for this organization. So, have you been keeping tabs on us, Professor Corbin?"

I shook my head. "Actually, I'm just learning about you guys. I tried to do a little research before I got here, but I must have gotten the names confused. I was a high school teacher not too long ago, so I know how difficult it can be working with kids. I heard about the good you and your partners have done in the city, so I wondered if you had any use for an educator like me on the staff? Strictly on a voluntary basis, of course."

"Interesting," Lockwell said, staring at me as if to size up my qualifications. "Mr. Corbin, you do realize that our approach to reaching these troubled youths is heavily dependent on religion. Exactly how do you feel about the mixture of academia and religion?"

My lips contorted as I smirked and said, "Well, Pastor, that's a loaded question if I've ever heard one, but it just so happens that I'm somewhat of an expert on religious history and ancient cultures. In other words, I have no issue with religion if it provides the means to necessitate change. I don't have to agree with everything if the purpose is simply to save the lives of children."

Lockwell paused and stared at me. I shifted with awkwardness and waited for the pastor to respond.

"I ask because I'm sure you're aware of the zealot who has recently plagued the city with violence? I'm talking about the religious murders. I only mention it because there were once three of us running this organization. One of us fell victim to that murderer. Now, as you already know, there are only two of us left. Speaking of the two of us, here is someone I think you've been wanting to meet walking up now," Lockwell said as his partner appeared from inside.

"Nicholas, I'd like you to meet Professor James Corbin. James, this is Deacon Nicholas Bianchi of St. Mark's Catholic Church and my partner of this foundation."

Deacon Bianchi climbed the stairs and walked toward me with an unnatural smile on his face. The kind of smile someone gives when they are forced to be in professional photographs.

"Buonasera, Signore Corbin. It's a pleasure to meet you. Thank you for celebrating God's cause with us. What are you a professor of, exactly?" Deacon Bianchi said as he extended his hand to greet me.

Lockwell smiled at me and said, "Gentlemen, I'll let you two get acquainted. I have plenty of young men and women who can use some guidance right now."

Pastor Lockwell hurried as if he couldn't get away from Bianchi fast enough, and left me in the presence of the man I had been so anxious to meet.

Just the sight of Bianchi stirred the beast within me, but I shook his hand and gave him a fake smile I had practiced so many times before.

"I'm a Professor of Ancient Cultures and Religious History, Deacon. I have to say, I admire the work you're doing here. I would like to be a part of it," I said, answering Bianchi's question.

"Ah, a topic near and dear to my heart. Thank you for your acknowledgement of our small accomplishments here. If we can bring one troubled youth to God, it is worth it all," Bianchi said, staring at me with eyes drained of emotion, as if to size me up and intimidate me. "Why do you want to be a part of this movement, Professor?"

I stepped closer to Bianchi and glared back at him. He did not give an inch of ground.

"Deacon, I want you to understand something, and I'm not here to waste any time," I replied in a hushed tone. "I know who and *what* you are. Unfortunately for you, you murdered someone I valued dearly. Fortunately for me, I found you. You have no idea the grave mistake you've made, but I promise that you will find out soon."

Deacon Bianchi's eyes widened slightly, but after a brief pause, a crooked smile spread across one side of his face.

"Professor, I am a man of God. I'm not quite sure what you are referring to, but I would appreciate it if you would leave. This is no place for violence or threats," Bianchi replied.

"Is that right, Deacon? Is that your play? Coyness? You are committing murders around this city. Those acts are anything but coy, Deacon. All for some foolish religious cause? Fuck your coyness. You killed Priestess Nadia!"

A burning desire to kill surged through my veins, and Bianchi flinched at the yellow glow that flickered in my eyes.

He stepped back from me and sighed.

"Professor, let's say for the sake of argument I am the man you say I am. It is my understanding she was an idolator. It seems she had it coming," Bianchi said. "Again, hypothetically speaking, if I was the man you think I am, then my charge isn't over. You just showed me the demon within you. And if I was that man, I couldn't allow something like you to continue to feast on the people of New Orleans. Priestess Nadia, her throat was slit, wasn't it? The same blade I used to slice her throat open, I would use to cut out your demon heart. Again, hypothetically, of course."

Rage bubbled inside me so much that I couldn't contain the start of my transformation. My fingernails turned as black as tar as they morphed into sharp claws, and my bare skin on my hand turned to leathery flesh.

I breathed deep to prevent the beast from consuming me, but Bianchi noticed the change in my hands and continued to grin.

"I never mentioned how she was killed, Deacon. I don't think you are talking in hypotheticals any longer," I said, still anxious to spill his blood.

"James, we are past hyperbole. I've been looking for you, devil; thank you for making this easy," Bianchi said. "Now is not our time. Today, I am here to do God's work. By the way, no matter how hard the Priestess tried, the blood spilling from Nadia's throat kept her from screaming."

I glanced around the yard and watched the families enjoying themselves, unaware of the two monsters that stood a few feet away.

I turned back to Bianchi and scowled. "I'll see you soon."

"I look forward to it, James."

CHAPTER THIRTY

"There will be no light."
—Goliath

━━━━━━━━━━━━━━━━━━━━━━━━━━━━━━━━

Detective Maor slammed the door shut behind her and slid the dead bolt into place. She sat at the wooden desk near the kitchen in her apartment, pushed the bottle of vodka aside, and slammed the book on the surface, as she tried her best to catch her breath after her escapade to James' house.

"What the fuck are you hiding, James?" Maor mumbled, examining the carved symbols on the book.

Maor paid more attention to the symbol also etched onto James' chest and painted on his floor, causing a shiver to turn her skin cold with unease.

The worn edges of the book and the faded pages made it look visibly old, and Maor assumed it would be written in some sort of an ancient language, but when she opened the first page, she raised her brow in surprise.

It's plain English, Maor observed. *And it reads as if it were written for a high school student.*

As the minutes ticked by, Maor learned the history of Zoroastrianism and its influence in ancient Persia. Her disgust grew with the vile tales of powerful men who committed despicable acts in the name of the symbols of illumination and destruction.

Thousands of years have passed, and mankind hasn't grown, Maor thought as painful childhood memories filled her mind.

Maor stroked the leather cover and restudied the symbols on the front. From reading the book, she had discovered that James wore Ahriman's symbol of destruction on his chest, which represented the worst aspects of man and its tainted blood.

"Tainted blood? I know another name for evil when I see it," she said, and she proceeded to read from the book. *"The sin of man feeds the growth of Ahriman; the birth of the essence was his most depraved act. The essence was awarded to the most desperate of man and enhanced the personal beast or demon that may have laid dormant within him. Whatever its charge by Ahriman, it feeds both the essence within and Ahriman himself, making the beast stronger until all humanity is lost."*

As the words resonated in her head, her legs quivered under the desk and she dreaded what James could have done.

He said he didn't get help for his depression. He just took care of it, she thought.

Maor crossed her arms and rested her head on the desk.

The thought of monsters and gods overwhelmed Maor after stealing the book and learning some of the most disturbing parts of history, but the stillness of the room calmed her.

But as Maor closed her eyes, a shrill screech against one of the windowpanes disturbed her peace and startled her.

Maor lifted her head and listened to the continuous screech. She stood from the table and rushed over to the window in her bedroom, only to stare out into the dark neighborhood. She pressed her forehead against the glass for a better look outside, when an object struck the center of the window, creating the same high-pitched screech.

Alarmed, Maor squinted into the black abyss and heard a low growl from the other side of the window. She stepped away as her heart pounded and two yellow eyes appeared before her. The yellow glow intensified, and the rumbling growl shook the glass panes.

"What the hell?!" Maor shouted as a giant beast emerged from the darkness.

Filthy black claws scratched the glass and a monstrous face with large teeth glowered at the detective. Maor's entire body froze, and the creature let out a sinister laugh as it watched her in terror.

"Nola," the beast said with a grin.

"G-Goliath?" Maor stuttered, but before she could say anything

more, the monster smashed through the window, sending shards of glass throughout the bedroom.

Maor screamed as the sharp fragments cut into her skin and fresh blood trickled down her limbs. She turned to escape Goliath as he landed in her room, but the monster's claws grabbed the back of her neck, stopping her in her tracks.

Goliath lifted her from the floor to bring her to eye level, and Maor's feet dangled and swung around in a frenzied panic. She tried to punch and pound Goliath's muscular chest with a balled fist, but Goliath's strength overpowered her.

"There will be no light," Goliath growled as his grip tightened.

Maor gasped for air and said, "W-what l-light?"

As Goliath continued to squeeze her neck, her bones snapped and the life in her eyes drifted away. Her lifeless body thumped against the floor and Goliath's laughter filled the room.

"NO!" Maor yelled, raising her sweaty head from the table.

Her shallow breathing panicked her more as she scanned around her room with fear, but she soon realized that everything had been a dream.

Maor exhaled with relief and guzzled a couple more shots of vodka as she revisited the last page of James' book. She reread the final line and furrowed her brow.

What does it all mean? she wondered. *What light?*

CHAPTER THIRTY-ONE

"If I can't find him, I'll let him find me."
—James Corbin

The aroma of the fresh coffee filled The Redd Bean as it did every morning.

It was another bustling workweek for the patrons who shuffled in and out, but not for me.

Spilling Deacon Bianchi's blood had been one of the only things I could focus on, so I had taken the time off work to avoid being delayed or distracted. I shifted my shoulders sitting in the chair, as I pulled at my clothes, still uncomfortable in my own skin; a more frequent occurrence. The only comfort I felt was when I was in the form of the beast; the only satisfaction was blood, any blood. It felt natural. It felt right.

After popping up at S.H.A.P.E., Bianchi had disappeared, so I had visited his church, apartment, and headquarters again, but still, he hid himself well.

After finishing the last of my coffee, with a smile, I raised my mug in the air to get the attention of Donna, the Redd's daughter, behind the counter.

Donna met my gaze, waved enthusiastically, and approached the table with an innocent brightness in her eyes and a sweet smile.

"Still hangin' out, James?" Donna said in a snarky tone. "You've been in here just about every day this week. I'm not complaining because my family could always use the business, but don't you have a job to go to?"

I gave her an icy stare cold enough to turn the hot coffee to ice and scoffed. "You're a smart girl, Donna. I know a little witty banter is part of our routine when we see each other. Not today. Don't concern yourself with grown folk affairs. Just pour the coffee."

Donna nodded as her eyes glazed over with tears. "Fair enough, Mr. Corbin."

She refilled my cup and hurried back to the counter, leaving me at my table as a news broadcast from the TV filled the café.

"Again, we have breaking news," the reporter announced. "New Orleans Police are looking for community leader and activist, Deacon Nicholas (David) Bianchi. He is wanted for questioning regarding several ongoing murder investigations. If you see or hear from Deacon Bianchi, please contact the New Orleans Police Department via the hotline number or contact Lead Detective Nola Maor of the First Precinct."

Bianchi's face on the screen made me realize that everyone in the city would be on the lookout for him, so I had even less time to deal with him myself.

"If Nola is onto him, it won't be much longer before he's in custody," I muttered to myself as a fresh wave of rage surged through me.

Out of nowhere, I slammed my fist onto the wooden table and accidentally split it in half. The patrons nearby screamed with fright and the Redd family glowered in my direction.

"James, what the hell is wrong with you? Get outta here, and don't come back!" Mr. Redd yelled across the café.

I scoffed and stood from my seat with a slight smile on my face. "Whatever."

I charged out of the café, every cell in my body tingling with agitation, and sprinted across the street to the wait station of the St. Charles streetcar line.

The enjoyment I felt as I watched the various people walk by or stand next to me as we awaited the arrival of the streetcar aroused every fiber of the hunter within me.

"If I were a well-known pillar in the community and a so-called man of God, where would I hide?" I asked myself as the streetcar arrived. "The news broadcast will only send him underground, but he's not likely to leave the city. He wants to hunt as well."

The smell of the different passengers on the streetcar reminded me of the smell of a butcher shop upon entering. The scent of the various fleshy bodies made me look forward to my next kill.

"Maor will be his target now, if she hasn't been already..." I mumbled, drawing attention from the other passengers, as I tapped the metal handlebar. The gaze of the other passengers reminded me that the slightest noise in such a closed area garnered attention. That's when it hit me. "If I can't find him, I'll let him find me."

CHAPTER THIRTY-TWO

"You speak of the cleansing, Father?"
—Deacon Bianchi

The wanted posters that displayed his face everywhere filled him with dread and irritation, but he took the opportunity to hide in plain sight. Everyone would have expected him to leave town, so skulking next to the building that housed dozens of investigative journalists was the best disguise.

The merriment of young adults carried through the empty halls of the abandoned house across from the historically black Catholic University, but once the party came to an end an hour or so later, Bianchi slipped out the front door and made his way onto the sidewalk unnoticed.

Bianchi's temporary denim overalls and white T-shirt made him appear as any other handyman in the city.

A group of students strolled toward him, and his usual instinct to greet them with the word of the Lord would not be in his best interest. He had to keep to himself and stick to the shadows. Besides, none of the students paid any attention to him or the news. Most were self-involved and preoccupied with school, parties, or impressing someone of the opposite sex to quench their carnal desires.

Bianchi continued along the campus until his walk brought him to the steps of the university's church. An old, decrepit building, but still used to service the many Catholic students on campus.

Simply being near the service of his God gave Bianchi

peace. However, he knew his moments of peace were fleeting. Even dressed down as a handyman, sitting out in the open offered *some* risk, but Bianchi didn't mind getting caught as long as he hunted Detective Maor and James Corbin first.

Bianchi perched on the front steps of the church and observed more students as they wandered by.

The variety of behavior amongst them amused Bianchi. Regardless of their sinful activities on occasion, these children had made it to the next stage of their lives. Some from the very neighborhoods that tried to end their lives.

"God's work," he said, beaming. "But there is more work to be done." Bianchi rose to his feet and clutched the falcata blade tucked in his pants. He sighed with relief at the thought of ending her sinful life when a deep voice spoke, catching his attention.

"Can I help you?"

Bianchi looked over his shoulder and saw a tall, slender man in a black cassock with a yellow stole. The man was clean shaven and neat in his appearance, but his eyes were red, as if he had finished crying.

"Hello, Father. I was resting and enjoying the night air. I am a man of faith and I enjoy being near the church," Bianchi said, attempting to appear as normal as possible. "I'll be on my way, Father."

The priest dipped his bushy brow and squinted at Bianchi. "Wait. Don't I know you from somewhere?"

"Yes, Father. I'm a handyman here on campus. You may have seen me around before."

"Italian accent, I see. I'm a fan of your country's culture and history, but I'm not sure the university is where I know you from," the priest said. "Oh well, it doesn't matter right now with all that's going on in this city. I'm happy to talk to someone who is a fan of the church these days. But I suppose the number of deaths surrounding the city has caused many to lose their faith."

"You speak of the cleansing, Father?" Bianchi asked.

"Cleansing? No. I speak about the murders committed in the Lord's name," the priest corrected. "It's reprehensible. Now, tonight to lose another man of the cloth... We need God more than ever in this city."

"I'm sorry, Father; another?" Bianchi inquired, trying to hide his anger from the priest's comments.

"Yes. Unfortunately, Father Donovan from St. Mark's here in the city has been murdered," the priest informed. "We met a couple of times a few years back. He was a kind man, and the embodiment of what we all strive to be as servants of the Lord. Not only was he murdered, but the police suspect it was that monster Goliath. First, the news of the Deacon evading police, and now this. It's terrible."

"F-Father Donovan is dead?" Bianchi stuttered with shock.

His face reddened with fury and he squeezed the handle of the hidden blade.

"You knew him? I'm sorry. I would have broken the news with more care," the priest said apologetically.

"No, I did not know him!" Bianchi yelled. "I hate to hear about such violence against men of faith."

The priest raised his brow at the handyman's emotional response, but after a brief pause, he narrowed his eyes with suspicion.

"I still feel as though I know you from somewhere, sir. What did you say your name was again?"

"I didn't!" Bianchi snapped, staring into the priest's innocent eyes. "Goodnight, Father."

Bianchi turned on his heel and charged away from the priest, trying to get out of sight as fast as possible.

"Goodnight to you as well," the priest replied as Bianchi hurried back toward the southern part of the campus.

Deacon Bianchi arrived back at his abandoned hideout and changed into a set of dark clothes. He shoved the blade into his bag and slung it across his shoulder.

James Corbin's actions were an affront to God and a slight to Bianchi. Father Donovan had always been a true man of the Lord, and he had accepted Bianchi when he arrived from Italy to America.

Mr. Corbin isn't a demon, after all; he's the devil himself, Bianchi thought. *He must die.*

CHAPTER THIRTY-THREE

"I've been waiting for you."
—Goliath

During the hours that passed, up on the school rooftop directly across the street, I kept an eye on the back of St. Mark's Church as dusk descended on the city and my hunger for Bianchi's blood kept me on the edge of the change. Since Nadia's death, my focus on finding him could not be shaken.

I peered over the ledge and kept my eye on the undercover cop car that had been parked near the end of the block for a short while. A dark silhouette sat inside and observed the church.

As I noticed the light that flashed on inside the window of the church's sacristy, I stood, and the beast forced its way out of me.

Fully transformed, I leapt from the roof and landed on the sidewalk below. I scanned the surroundings and darted across the street, only to rip through the fence with my razor-sharp claws. I advanced through the dark parking lot and bounded onto the roof of the church; the perfect place to attack Bianchi no matter which exit he used.

Inside the church, Bianchi made his way through the dark sacristy to a little-known door that led to his apartment, but as he entered, he froze at the sight of the room completely ransacked and in disarray.

"No doubt done by those damn scavengers," Bianchi spat. "Detective Maor with the warrant, I'm sure. A thorn in my side. Slitting her throat will be sweet."

Bianchi had only returned to the church to retrieve a precious item and discover what had happened to Father Donovan, but only in that order. If he had to scarper before he could enter Donovan's chambers, then so be it.

Bianchi grabbed a black duffel bag and some clothes from his closet and reached for the item he had returned for: a silver box he kept hidden at the back on the floor.

The lid of the box had been flipped open, and Bianchi huffed at the thought of some meathead in a uniform touching and violating something so sacred.

He caressed the box with his fingers and grabbed the old Bible from inside, holding it to his lips and saying a brief prayer.

As he opened the Bible and touched the handwritten words scribed on the inside cover, memories of where he found his calling flooded his mind.

"Ah... Poggioreale Prison. How can something so beautiful come from such a vile place?" Bianchi said, putting the Bible back into the box and then into the bag.

Bianchi grabbed his bag and headed back into the main room of the church.

As he advanced toward Father Donovan's sleep chambers, he noticed a lengthy strip of caution tape that blocked off the red door ahead. Bianchi snatched the tape down and pushed through the door before him, dreading what could have been inside.

The red stains and splintered furniture throughout the room made Deacon Bianchi blink the tears away as best he could as he imagined the suffering Father Donovan must have experienced.

"Father Donovan was a true servant; he did not deserve this," Bianchi said, slamming the door to the chambers.

Bianchi charged back through the church and into the side alley as pain from his loss coursed through his mind and soul. He bent over to catch his breath and wiped the sweat from his brow, thinking of his next move.

"I'm through hiding and welcome anyone to cross my path," he said, eager to leave the church and his loss behind him. "There is no need for me to hunt any of them down. If I make myself known, they'll come to me."

Once Bianchi caught his breath, he approached the illuminated exit sign above the door and sighed with relief, but when he glanced up at the night sky, his heart plummeted at the sight of a beastly figure on the roof.

"I've been waiting for you," the beast growled, leaping down from the roof and standing before Bianchi.

Bianchi squared his shoulders and smiled at the monster with a racing heart. He dropped his bag onto the damp concrete and pulled the Falcata blade from his waist, holding it by his side. The handle pulsated in his hand as if it *wanted* the confrontation with the beast, filling Bianchi with unexpected confidence.

"What you did to Father Donovan was evil, beast. Like the others I've killed before you, you are an affront to God, demon!" Bianchi yelled through the alleyway.

Goliath sneered and jumped onto the side of the building, charged along the brick wall on all fours; its claws ripped through the brick violently. Its speed forced Bianchi to sidestep and retreat in the opposite direction, but the beast leapt after Bianchi and swung for his throat. Bianchi dropped to his knees to evade the beast's arm and lifted the blade above his head. He slashed Goliath across the chest and its blood splattered across his pale face.

Goliath roared into the air and put pressure on the wound as Bianchi looked on with a proud smile.

"One true God," Bianchi lectured, and he charged toward the beast.

Goliath leaped to its feet and lunged at Bianchi, grabbing him by the throat this time and lifting him from the ground. The beast sliced straight through Bianchi's arm and Bianchi wailed with agony, but Goliath wasn't done with him yet. The beast struck Bianchi's lower abdomen and launched him across the alleyway by the skin of his neck. Bianchi's limp body smacked the brick wall and thumped to the ground, blood pouring out onto the concrete.

Goliath let out a sinister laugh and glared at Bianchi's dead corpse.

"For the Priestess," the beast growled.

Goliath dipped its claws into Bianchi's blood and painted a message along the brick wall of the church.

The beast would have admired the wall a little longer, but the fresh chest wound seared with pain, and a voice from the other end of the alleyway caught Goliath off guard.

"James!"

The beast turned with a start and spotted the source of the voice, but it leaped onto the church roof and scarpered into the night.

Detective Maor froze and watched the beast retreat from the scene. As it disappeared into the darkness, she looked over at the gruesome sight of Deacon Bianchi.

Maor watched the blood trickle from his body to her polished army boots, and she followed the bloody stream to his corpse.

The brick wall dripped with blood, but Maor managed to make out a familiar message left by Goliath.

One True God.

CHAPTER
THIRTY-FOUR

"It's always evil."
—Detective Maor

Only a few minutes earlier, the alleyway of St. Mark had been occupied with two of the most vicious murderers in the city, but now, only one remained.

Given the blood that had been spilled in the city, one would assume Detective Maor would be elated at Deacon Bianchi's death, but frankly, she had grown tired of seeing blood, no matter the victim.

The blood in the alleyway pooled into the divot in the concrete and Deacon Bianchi's lifeless body lay in the fetal position against the brick wall. His intestines spilled out onto the ground and his severed arm still grasped the Falcata blade.

The emergency lights of the police squad cars illuminated the brick wall and brightened the message the beast had left behind.

"A literal mark of the beast," Detective Maor said, shaking her head in disbelief.

She dreaded how the brass would feel about a murderous deacon dead in the alleyway of a Catholic Church, but at least one of humanity's problems had been dealt with. Maor knew the Catholic community would forever gossip of Bianchi's murder, trying to frame the story to suit them, but the truth would always lie in the alleyway beside the church: a serial killer killed by another serial killer, in the dark with no witnesses.

"Just know that I got to you first. I knew who and what you really were," she whispered into Bianchi's ear as she stooped to his level.

"Detective Maor!" a uniformed officer shouted from the other end of the alley. "Brass! Incoming!"

Maor looked up and noticed Chief Martel and Deputy Chief Winslow marching toward her in smart attire with bright smiles on their faces, an unusual thing to do at a murder scene.

"Hello, sirs," Maor greeted with a raised eyebrow. "Given the look on your faces, I take it someone advised you of the victim already?"

"That mutha fucka never looked better!" Chief Martel said, forcing Maor to snigger with shock.

Chief Martel's propensity to overcompensate with foul language had become well-known throughout the police department, but one would think that a man at the top of the political food chain would be a little more buttoned up, so to speak.

"What happened here, Detective?" Deputy Chief Winslow asked, ignoring the chief's unprofessionalism.

Detective Maor exhaled and recalled everything that happened from the minute she pulled up in her car to the moment she watched Goliath flee the scene.

"Sir, if you don't mind, we might want to change the facts on the events a bit. I'd rather go with an officer involved in a shooting as a result of some good police work," Deputy Chief Winslow proposed with a nervous grin.

"Excuse me, Winslow?" Chief Martel exclaimed, mildly outraged.

"Think about it, sir," Deputy Chief Winslow pressed. These murders have frustrated the entire city, and the people have lost trust in you and the department, so they are about ready to run us out of town. If one of our officers took down a serial killer off the back of a city hall and department plan, the people's confidence in us would increase and they would also feel a little safer. We make Detective Maor the hero, and then announce our plan to hunt the monster and take back the streets from the drug dealers."

Chief Martel stared at Bianchi's body and contemplated Winslow's plan.

"That's fucking brilliant, Winslow," he said, beaming at his colleague and patting him on the back.

Their laughter echoed through the alleyway and Chief Martel turned to Detective Maor.

"Detective, I'm going to send another homicide detective this way to write this up, just as I said it happened. Internal Affairs will give you a call in the morning, so you need to tell them everything you told us. Except, when you ran to the alleyway for the arrest, Deacon Bianchi charged at you with that God awful, ugly blade. Panicked, you put one round in his chest and two in his arm. Do you understand me, Detective?" Chief Martel ordered, staring at her with intensity. "Internal Affairs is my old unit, and we go back quite a ways, so I'm going to give their captain a call right now to ensure that he understands how I want this to go. Just make your statement like I told you and you'll end up with a goddamn medal. You got me?"

"But sir, Goliath *gutted* him. I didn't fire my weapon, and he's not sh—"

"Let me worry about the details, Detective," Chief Martel interrupted. "You say what I tell you to say, and you'll be a city hero—again. Deputy, get on the horn with the FBI and advise them that we won't be needing their services. With Bianchi out of the picture, we can refocus our manpower to capturing that vicious animal out there."

Maor glanced from the chief to the deputy as her stomach twisted with discomfort and guilt over the lie she would soon be involved in.

The chief grabbed his radio and said, "Car 2 to dispatch."

"Yes, Car 2. Go 'head," the dispatcher answered.

"Ma'am, can you get Detective Raymond out here? We have an officer involved in a shooting and I need him as lead. 10-4?"

"10-4," she replied.

Maor's attention turned to James Corbin and how to reach him as fast as possible. She didn't fully understand his connection to the beast, and she needed answers before he killed again.

"Sir, do you mind if I go to my car and get something to drink? All of this has left me a little shaken," Detective Maor asked.

"Sure, but no alcohol," the chief replied.

Maor nodded and headed back to her car with weak legs and a pounding heart.

She had never presented herself as a scared little woman before, but given that the brass knew her *actual* encounter with the beast, they would have hardly expected her to be okay, so Maor used it to her advantage to get out of the alleyway and find James.

While Chief Martel and Deputy Chief Winslow remained in the alley to refine the details of their unethical and illegal plan, Maor slipped into her car and raced away from the scene.

As Maor sped through the different neighborhoods, images of Goliath up close flashed through her mind and filled her with fear.

She didn't want to accept that James had anything to do with the murders in the city, but after seeing the inverted symbol on the beast's chest, how could she ignore the truth?

Jesus, what am I gonna do? Maor wondered, her fingers trembling on the steering wheel. *Ancient deities, essence demons, and blood sacrifices; this can't be real life.*

Maor recalled the information she read in James' book, and she realized that none of it could be brushed off as fictional religious folklore. The thought of it all had Maor's head spinning.

Angra Mazda, Ahriman, the essence; it's all real. James is Goliath, Maor thought as she turned into James' neighborhood. *It's always pain and suffering. It's always evil. Where's the good? Where's the balance?*

Detective Maor pulled up to James' home and jumped out of the car. She drew her gun from her side holster and ran to the front door as if she were already chasing someone. She took a few deep breaths to prepare herself when chunks of wood flew past her head.

Maor ducked to avoid the splinted shrapnel and a massive figure lunged at her; its knee struck her shoulder and knocked her down the stairs. She smacked the back of her head on the ground and her gun slid across the walkway.

Goliath leapt from the roof of the house and landed inches from Maor's head, startling her into a shrill scream. She thought Goliath would take the opportunity to stamp on her head or rip her heart out, but as she lay on the ground, the beast scarpered toward the central part of the city.

Maor struggled to her feet and grabbed the back of her head, but her vision blurred, and a wave of dizziness overwhelmed her.

Trying to ignore the mild concussion symptoms, she grabbed her gun from the pavement and regained her bearings the best she could. She hopped back into her car and slammed the gas pedal, causing the screeching tires to echo through the night air.

Maor flew through each street, sped through red lights, and ran stop signs, forcing her to sideswipe a nearby car and dodge potential collisions from each intersection.

As Maor turned off the main road and approached City Park, she slowed her speed and gazed up at the large oak trees and banner of lights that arched above her head. If the beast had made it into the park, Maor had a huge problem on her hands. Not only did the park stretch for acres, but the museums, shops, and tall structures attracted all sorts of people. An ideal place for Goliath to hide—and kill.

With that in mind, Maor considered each factor of her surroundings as she idly drove through the park's narrow roads. She kept her wide eyes peeled as she steadied her breathing, when a young lady appeared from the darkness with tears in her eyes.

"Stop!" the distressed woman yelled, thumping her hands onto the hood of Maor's car.

The young lady's visible terror forced Maor out of her car.

"I-it's in the trees!" the woman said, pointing to a cluster of oak trees ahead.

Maor expected the woman to seek refuge in her car, but instead, she turned away from the detective and sprinted away from the trees, leaving her alone once again. Maor drew her gun and stared up into the canopy, narrowing her eyes and watching the branches sway from side to side.

The darkness hindered her vision, but the rustling leaves from all directions made her erratically point her weapon in case the beast leapt from the foliage.

After considering that Goliath had hidden somewhere else in the park, the beast bounded from the trees directly above Maor and shoved her onto the ground.

Somehow, she managed to hold onto her gun, but the sight of the muscular monster before her made her question whether her epoxy bullets would do anything.

As Maor rose to her feet and stared at the beast with wavering hands and weak knees, she noticed a gaping wound that stretched across its chest next to the inverted symbol. A wound like that would surely put anyone down permanently, but Goliath continued to bare its teeth at Maor, completely unfazed.

"James," Maor said in a soft tone, hoping to reach him.

The beast grinned wider and pushed Maor to the ground again, sending her sliding into the dirt across the dead fallen leaves. Goliath bellowed with laughter and skulked toward the detective, clutching its chest this time as if to acknowledge the pain.

Maor reluctantly raised her gun and fired two shots at the monster's legs, but the wounds healed immediately and the beast continued to prowl toward her. She gaped with disbelief and pulled the trigger again, firing two more rounds at its stomach. The shots hit Goliath in the lower abdomen, and one round hit him in the open wound from Bianchi's blade. Again, Goliath's abdomen healed, but the shot that pierced the wound forced the beast onto its knees in excruciating pain.

Maor leapt back up and pointed her weapon at the beast again, but before she could injure it further, Goliath growled and lunged at her, its claws piercing her left shoulder and spinning her around. The beast tore down her back and clawed her from the top of the shoulder blade to her kidney.

Maor's gun fell from her hand and she hit the ground, lying face down in the dirt. Blood splattered the leaves on the ground and the beast roared into the air, clutching its chest and writhing in pain.

The police sirens sounded in the distance and Goliath hobbled deeper into the park. Maor's eyes wavered as she moaned in pain and fell unconscious.

CHAPTER
THIRTY-FIVE

"I'm not going back!"
—James Corbin

The police likely wouldn't look for me in St. Louis Cemetery near Esplanade Ave., so their cars and sirens didn't concern me. Besides, given the pain that surged through my chest, the cemetery may have been the right place for me.

As I crumpled on the ground against a concrete tomb, searing pain in my chest worried me, especially since only my head and left side had changed back to human form. Could Bianchi's blade have done that? It came from Priestess Nadia, after all.

The gash had weakened me to the brink of death, leaving me struggling to breathe and wheezing, unable to fight my way out or change back. The strength the beast brought me had faded, and the excruciating pain did nothing but drain me even more as each second passed.

I remembered that feeling well from before Ahriman helped me. The sharp stomach pains from stress. The dull ache from migraines and anxiety attacks. The inability to get out of bed each morning. And the panic at the thought of speaking to anyone for long periods of time.

Just like this wound, all of that crippled me.

I'm not going back! I refused in my mind. *I can't go back!*

I clutched my chest yet again and squeezed my blood from the incision, roaring with agony. With one claw, I traced the mark of

Ahriman onto the ground and thought back to how much I enjoyed killing Father Donovan. I had no personal vendetta against him, he was just a body who had the blood I needed. My humanity did not obstruct me.

"My work is not done. Let me keep the power, and you can have my humanity," I pleaded, and a croaky voice called over to me.

"Mr., who are you talking to? Are you okay? What the hell!"

I looked up and spotted a frail old man a few meters away from me; his eyes wide from the blood and my failed transformation.

The man's overalls were covered in dirt and his shoes were falling apart. He backed away with a broom in hand, but tripped and fell over the raised concrete behind him.

I crawled toward the man and winced as the pain continued to torture me.

"Please, help me. Don't be scared. It did this to me," I pleaded.

"Mr., what are you? What happened to your body?" the man asked, slowly getting to his feet.

"It did this to me. It hurts. Help me!" I begged, crawling closer.

The man paused with a frown, but after a moment, he edged closer to me and bent over to examine the wound in my chest. He may have had the compassion to help me, but I didn't give him the chance.

I reached out with my beastly claws and tore open his throat. The man struggled for air as blood poured from the gaping hole, and his eyes stared into an empty void as he plummeted to the ground.

"Take it all!" I yelled.

Seconds after the death of the old man, my bloody chest healed like magic and the bones in my face shattered and reformed. The skin on my left side blistered as my massive arms reshaped themselves, and gloopy saliva dripped from my sharp teeth. A mixture of blood and adrenaline rushed through me and the strength the beast had given me returned.

The murder of the old man sealed the blood oath with Ahriman. I was no longer a broken man, and my humanity no longer existed.

I growled with satisfaction, and my yellow eyes illuminated the body before me. Then, everything went black.

CHAPTER THIRTY-SIX

"There is more to it than flesh and bone."
—Detective Maor

The blinding white light that hovered over Detective Maor's head intensified the pounding in her head. The muddled voices in the distance pushed her to open her eyes, hoping to identify who spoke and where she had been taken.

As she peeled open her eyes and blinked rapidly, Maor regained some focus, but her dry mouth prevented her from yelling out into the room.

The intense smell of rubbing alcohol and the cold metal rods bumping against her arms clarified her whereabouts. Plus, a large black man in a NOPD class A uniform stood before her.

Jesus, he loves that uniform, Maor thought.

Maor scanned the room for others who might have been there, but the only people present were Chief Martel and the nurse, who changed the IV bag.

Of course, who else would be there? Maor had no friends, no boyfriend, no husband, no one. No one but a sister who had always been as committed to her job as her. At least she had made the time to start a family. This close encounter with death reminded Maor that although she was young, she needed to make time to build a family.

As Maor glanced from the chief to the nurse, images of her fight with Goliath flickered through her memories. There is nothing like a near death experience to bring a little clarity.

"Water, please," Maor croaked.

"Hey! Detective. You're awake!" the chief cried with excitement in his tone.

"Chief, did we get him?" Maor asked.

"Straight to the point, I see," he replied.

Maor tried to sit up in anticipation, but the pain from her back pulsated through her body and brought tears to her eyes. She grunted and adjusted her body's position in the hospital bed.

"Easy. Easy, Detective Maor. You were injured pretty bad. I have to say, I can't believe you went toe to toe with that monster! You're one tough woman," the chief said with a rare smile.

"Cop," she corrected.

The chief raised an eyebrow. "Excuse me?"

"One tough cop."

"Ah, yes. One tough cop," the chief replied, beaming even brighter.

Maor gave him a quick smile before she returned to the matter at hand. "Chief, did we get him?"

Chief Martel shook his head. "We didn't, but you must have wounded it. We found blood on the scene, and you had gunshot residue on your hand, along with several rounds missing from your gun clip."

"So, it got away," she said, defeated. "It's only been one night. It *has* to still be in the city. It doesn't leave its prey ali—"

"Detective," the chief interrupted, "you've been in Charity Hospital for six days. Those wounds on your back could have killed you. We've been looking for it since that night, but we've had to put the entire city on lockdown."

"Lockdown?" Maor blurted.

"Yes, and there is no way the Mayor or I will survive this politically, not that it matters anymore, but the official record involving you and Deacon Bianchi is exactly what we talked about the night he died. The fact that you gave chase to Goliath, fought, *and* wounded it the same night, only solidified that story. You have some awards coming your way."

"Sir, the awards are not important to me. This beast needs to be put down! I shot it four times, but it healed almost immediately. It only slowed down when I hit it in the open wound caused by Bianchi."

Detective Maor rested her head back on her pillow, already weak from her conversation with Chief Martel.

As she tried to gather herself, the nurse hurried back in with her water, which brought some much-needed relief to her sore throat.

"There is more to it than flesh and bone, Chief. It's something else; something different," Maor explained. "Obviously, it's not human, but it—it can't be hurt like a normal being."

"Are you sure, Detective?"

"Of course, I'm sure, Chief. I know what I saw."

"Detective, you have been in the hospital for six days. In that time, Goliath has killed seventeen citizens," he told her.

"What?!" Nola exclaimed.

"Yes, seventeen men, women, and children all across New Orleans," Chief Martel clarified. "At first, we thought it kept killing due to being injured, scrabbling to get somewhere to hide and heal, while taking out anyone who got in its way. Then, the bodies started stacking and there its killings lost a pattern."

Maor covered her mouth with shock. "Oh my God!"

"We've had several reports from people who have managed to shoot or cut the beast, but they have all given the exact same statement as you. The wounds heal and it just keeps coming. It has spoken once before it killed one victim, but all it said was, *'For Arman,'*" Chief Martel explained.

"Ahriman," Maor corrected.

Chief Martel nodded. "Maybe so. Sounds about right, but I would have to look at the report again. Does it mean anything to you?"

"No, sir, he said something similar to me before he sliced my back open," Maor stated.

Her attempt to cover the truth about James being Goliath resulted from her not accepting the situation, but from the sound of it, given the carnage, there wasn't much of James left.

"Detective, your sister is in town and has been in and out of here to see you. She's been spending most of her time poking around police headquarters, and the city for that matter, trying to hunt down the monster. She's just as tenacious as you. Pregnant and all, she's been hunting that bastard."

"I'm not surprised. It's something she can control. She would rather do that than sit here and watch me suffer. I'm sure she'll be by again soon," Maor replied.

"Well, the police Chaplin is here to see you. She's been here every day waiting for you to wake up. I'll be in touch again when you are feeling a little better," Chief Martel said. "We have to come up with a plan to catch this monster and your input would be invaluable. I'll leave you to your rest and talk to you soon, *Sergeant.*"

Chief Martel gave her a proud smile, and Maor took a few

moments to realize that she had been promoted in the six days she had been asleep.

"Chief, thank you for coming to see me. I know there are some political points to score with you being here, but it still matters that you actually showed up. Thank you for everything. I'll be back on my feet soon," Maor said.

"Still a straight shooter, I see. You're welcome, Detective. We'll talk soon."

Chief Martel left the hospital room and Maor took a deep breath as Police Chaplin Samantha Moss entered.

Maor rested the back of her head on her pillow again, anxious at the thought of another visitor. The last thing she wanted was to be in this hospital bed, even less so, talking with the police chaplin about faith.

Before Maor could put her feet on the expected cold hospital floor, the door opened and a familiar face that often had a presence at the First Precinct Station walked in.

"Hello, friend," Chaplin Samantha Moss greeted with an upbeat tone.

"Hey, Chaplin," Maor replied, incredulous that anyone could believe in God with everything going on in the city.

"How are you feeling, Nola?" chaplin Moss asked.

"I'm hanging in there, Chaplin. I just need to get back on my feet and put an end to all this bloodshed," Maor said.

"Always the tough girl. I can't say you are wrong. There is a lot of bloodshed on the streets, and too many people in pain. You do know that it's not solely your responsibility to stop it all, though, right?"

"You're right, Chaplin. Too much pain," Maor agreed but with a hostile tone. "Tell me, Chaplin, how do you feel about that? I mean, where is your God right now? Families are being torn apart, innocent people are dying, murders in the name of religion, and demon monsters running in the streets. It turns out all the religious fairytales are real this time. So, where is he?"

Chaplin Moss froze at Maor's outburst and stood with bulging eyes.

"Well, you've clearly been wanting to ask me that for a long time," Chaplin Moss assumed. "Look, Detective Maor, I'll admit the sight of that monster made me question some things, and the murders are disturbing. Obviously, there is something supernatural involved in this, but how did you conclude that it is a demon, specifically?"

Maor stared at Chaplin Moss, and realized that talking to

someone would help clear her head a bit.

As Chaplin Moss sat beside her bed, Maor opened up about her upbringing, relationship with the Catholic church, and the horrific incident she witnessed.

"I'm so sorry, Detective. I remember that scandal well, but I had no idea you *witnessed* that incident," Chaplin Moss said, her mouth agape with shock. "And now these murders years later by Deacon Bianchi; I can see why your faith is shaken."

"My faith is not shaken, Chaplin; it is broken. Now, with this goddamn beast here, I know there is a God. In fact, I know there are many gods. They just don't care," Maor spat.

Chaplin Moss furrowed her brow. "How do you know this, Detective? You said the beast was a demon. Where did you get this from?"

Maor sighed. "I found a book while visiting a friend at his home. It's called the *Book of Blood*, and it's about an ancient religion and its duality. The dark versus the light. Apparently, the book allows you to conjure an ancient evil deity called Ahriman. I guess if you make the right deal, it will give you some of its essence, a shard, if you will. That essence makes you part demon. That is what is killing people and I think my friend is dead because of it."

Maor glugged the rest of the water, her breathing labored, and Chaplin Moss sat in silence.

"So, Chaplin, like I asked you before, where is God now?"

"With everything you've been through, the only answer I have is—I don't know," the Chaplin answered.

Maor laughed at the Chaplin's answer and winced every time she had to take a deep breath.

"Detective Maor, you have always been a trustworthy person, but up until this point in my life, I've always believed my God is the only God. Now you're telling me other gods exist, but that doesn't matter to me. I still believe my God is the almighty," the Chaplin said. "I'm Protestant and you're Catholic, same God, different religion. That means my God is your God. Since that is the case, God has not forsaken you. He has been preparing you for this your entire life, and He has given you everything you need to be victorious."

"Oh, give me a fucking break!" Maor yelled. "Are you telling me that God has let all of these people die because of some divine plan? For me?"

"That's not what I'm saying at all," the Chaplin defended. "Our God prepares us for our challenges, and He provides everything we need to fight the battles ahead of us. Some require more faith than others. All your experiences until now have put you in a dark place, but you have grown into the powerful fighter you are now. Just like the book, you mentioned that the only way to fight the darkness, especially the monster, is to use light. Your spirit has to be in the light."

Maor rolled her eyes, but Chaplin Moss continued.

"I hate to recite scripture, but Ephesians 5:8 says, *'For at one time you were darkness, but now you are light in the Lord. Walk as children of light.'* Think of the lives you've saved *because* you are built the way you are, from your experiences. God has made you a detective. He is awaiting your return to the light. And if your book says what you said it did, then this beast is also walking in the darkness. It needs to be brought into the light. The light is cleansing, Detective. It is all-consuming."

Maor stared at the Chaplin as a smile crept onto her face and her muscles relaxed. It amazed her how this woman had been able to focus on her faith in a time when evil and blood were plentiful.

"Sam, call me Nola, please," Maor said. "I understand what you are saying. The duality of man is the same for gods. There is light and there is darkness. The only way to destroy the darkness is to bring it to the light. Sam, I don't agree with the way God does things, but maybe he brought you into my life for the conversation we are having today. Thank you, Sam, and sorry for snapping at you."

"I'm glad to be of service, Detec—umm, Nola. I'm sorry your past has failed you, but you can't let it consume you," Sam said. "Would you like for me to pass by tomorrow too? Charity Hospital isn't but a stone's throw away from the station."

"Yes," Maor replied. "I would like that."

"Okay, well you get some rest and I'll see you tomorrow, Nola," the Chaplin said.

As Chaplin Moss left the room, Maor changed the channel and stared at the TV, but the beast consumed her focus. The thought of Goliath on the streets for another night, hiding in the shadows, waiting to kill again, made Maor sick to her stomach, but a surge of determination coursed through her as she considered what had to be done.

"I'll bring the light to him."

CHAPTER THIRTY-SEVEN

"Come on, goddamn it! Let's end this!"
—Detective Maor

Maor walked into her chilled apartment and headed straight to her bedroom, throwing her keys and bag of prescriptions onto her bed.

She glanced over at the *Book of Blood* on her desk and reflected on her conversation with Chaplin Moss.

Maor had been anxious to discover if her hunch about the power of the light was right, but James' book couldn't help her now. Everything she desired was stashed away in her closet.

"Come on, you, we have some work to do," Maor said as she grabbed a 12-gauge pump-action shotgun from her closet.

The shotgun had been a present from her sister when she graduated from the police academy. Maor loved using it at the shooting range, the only place she could enjoy it properly without getting arrested.

She slung the weapon over her shoulder and winced in pain as it bounced against her wounded back. Maor poured and swallowed a couple of glasses of vodka from the bottle that sat on her night stand to help with the pain. She then stuffed a white T-shirt and a roll of duct tape into the smaller backpack at the bottom of the closet, which was already half full. The bag made a clanging noise as Maor placed it over her shoulder.

"It's time for my personal demon to lend a helping hand," she said, closing the door and rushing out of the room.

But when she reached the bedroom door, she stopped to make sure she had everything she needed. She noticed how clean her desk had stayed since she had been gone. Not a single piece of paper was out of place, yet something differed from a few minutes ago.

The Book of Blood had vanished.

Maor stared at the desk in disbelief but turned back and closed the door behind her.

"No explanation needed. I have stranger things to deal with."

She gathered her badge and radio, along with her service firearm, and firmly holstered it on her hip as she left her apartment. As she placed the shotgun and bag on the passenger side seat in her car, she switched on her police radio to hear the calls for service throughout the city.

Although she wasn't officially back on duty, she wanted to hunt tonight without any other obligations interfering. It was best for her to do this alone, especially outside the purview of her sister.

"As much as I could use her help, I can't put her and the baby at risk."

The police radio remained silent for most of her drive across the Crescent City Connection. The amount of murders Goliath had committed in the past ten days had caused the state government to force the city into lockdown with a mandatory curfew of 7:00 p.m. and the National Guard prowled the streets.

A couple of hours passed, and Detective Maor drove through most of New Orleans. As the beast had not made an appearance throughout her drive, she decided to venture to the more violent lower Ninth Ward.

From what she had heard, there were few sightings of Goliath in that part of the city, and it occurred to her that there used to be a place in the lower ninth that both Deacon Bianchi and James had in common. A location more meaningful to James in particular, so if he had any humanity left, it could have been a place Goliath visited.

With that in mind, Maor drove deeper into the lower Ninth Ward near the industrial canal and cruised along the desolate streets of various poor neighborhoods.

"In the Fifth District, signal 107, code 2, caller claims to have witnessed Goliath on the rooftop of a house near Jackson Barracks.

Caller stated it's sitting there waiting for something," the dispatcher said, startling Maor.

A string of officers replied to the dispatcher's call and headed in that direction, still itching to get justice for the injured detective.

If the beast had been sitting in that area, it wouldn't be anymore, and Maor didn't trust the suspicious person's call. Kids often placed those false calls to have a little fun at the police's expense. Besides, she couldn't have anyone know that she had embarked on her own hunt for Goliath.

As Maor pulled up in front of Priestess Nadia's old place, she rolled down the car windows to listen for any movement in the neighborhood. The sudden ringing of her cell phone invaded the night's silence and rattled her nerves.

Not now, sis. I know you are looking for me and as much as I could use your back-up, I can't put you in harm's way, Maor thought as she silenced the ring.

The eerie stillness of the darkened street gave Maor an uncomfortable feeling, but she couldn't let that stop her mission.

Detective Maor reached into the black backpack and grabbed the white T-shirt and duct tape, while keeping an eye on the window and door of the old Voodoo Emporium. She ripped the T-shirt into three large shreds and hauled three large bottles of vodka from the bag. Maor drank about a shot's worth from each to create a little room in the bottles.

"My demon," she slurred.

Maor dunked a shred of fabric into each bottle and repeated for each shred of fabric, ensuring the alcohol was absorbed on both ends. After she put a soaked piece of fabric back half way in each bottle, she heavily taped each of them so the rag would not slip back in or the vodka would not spill out. She set them next to her on the seat. She exited the car in a hazy state and grabbed her shotgun on the way out. She peered into the silent neighborhood and placed the items on the hood of the car. She secured the shotgun on her shoulder as haunting memories of the beast ripping her flesh filled her with fear.

The crackle of her police radio disrupted her unease and an officer on the call to Jackson Barracks informed dispatch that Goliath was nowhere to be found at the location.

"I knew it. Where are you?" Maor mumbled.

She edged a little closer to the house and peered into the window. The pitch-black darkness inside seemed to have moved slightly, but the shots of alcohol made her doubt her eyes.

"Damn it, Nola. You could have just poured a little out. Did you have to drink it?"

Straining her eyes to focus, to her horror, a pair of yellow eyes glowed and stared back at her from inside the house. Maor stood on the balls of her feet and pumped a shell into the chamber of the shotgun.

"I see you," she said, pointing the weapon at the window. "Come on, goddamn it! Let's end this!"

Maor advanced toward the house when the beast hurtled through the window and sent shards of glass flying toward her. She turned her head to protect her face and fired a shot toward the beast. The buckshot's whizzed from the short barrel and scattered across Goliath's face and chest.

The monster growled in pain and fell to the ground. It immediately jumped to its feet without a scratch.

Maor turned to load her shotgun again, but when she readied herself for another shot, Goliath had disappeared. She scanned the area with her gun, ready to fire, and spotted the monster on the roof of Nadia's home as it growled and bared its teeth. She fired another shot, but Goliath swiftly moved to the other side. The sound of the pump action echoed in the night as Maor fired a few more rounds, but only achieved the same results.

The beast jumped to the ground before the house and Maor fled to the hood of her car, seizing her lighter from her pocket on the way. She grabbed one of the Molotov cocktails and ignited the dangling cloth from the bottle.

The beast grinned as it watched and moved toward her with aggression. Maor threw the flaming bottle at Goliath, which forced the beast to dodge, and the glass smashed against Nadia's home. As the lethal concoction set the house ablaze, Maor pumped another round into the chamber and fired another shot before Goliath could attack her. The cluster of buckshots hit Goliath in the chest and the beast let out a shrill squeal but stood its ground.

The flames intensified and Goliath raced toward the levy wall a block away from the burning home. As it jumped over and headed into the abandoned area beneath the industrial canal bridge, Maor followed in her car and reloaded her shotgun when she arrived. She threw the bag of flammable liquid on her back and headed for Goliath.

The industrial canal had been littered with burned out abandoned cars, broken appliances, and sharp rocks; it was a hazardous environment and precarious place for the beast to hide.

As the bottles in her bag clanked about, Maor looked around for movement and pumped another round into her shotgun. She made her way under the bridge and her senses heightened.

The smell of the muddy water made her nauseous, and the deeper in she went, the more her body trembled. She knew that either herself or the beast would die, but she needed to try to kill it before it killed anyone else.

As she scanned her surroundings, keeping an eye out for the beast, a blaring horn from a passing barge jolted her to the bones, so much so that she failed to spot the beast among the trash.

Goliath laughed in the distance, and Maor fired at a burned-out car in a desperate attempt to silence the monster's taunts.

"Goliath, I know what you are. I know who you serve. You don't scare me," Maor challenged, removing the bottles from her bag and setting them on the ground before her. "That's right, beast. I know you serve Ahriman. I know you are filled with his darkness, and your pathetic mission is pain, fear, and blood. But I'm not scared of you. In fact, I'm pissed. You took a friend away from me. I could tell he was in pain, but he didn't need you. No one needs you. It's time for you to die!"

Maor glanced around in search of Goliath and fired more rounds into random areas, trying to flush out the beast. She noticed a nearby car move and kept her sight on that area.

"I have news for you, beast. I can help you. If there is any part of James left in you, it doesn't have to be the end. I can drive out the darkness. How does that sound?" she yelled into the night.

Maor dropped the bag and pulled out a bottle from inside. She ignited the rag with her lighter and tossed it at the car that moved, setting the vehicle alight. Maor reached for the last bottle and lit the second rag once again. The flames drove Goliath out from behind the car and the beast charged toward Maor, snarling with anger and hungry to dig its claws into her.

With a racing heart and a shrill scream, Maor launched the flaming bottle at the beast as it jumped toward her. The bottle met Goliath in the air and shattered on its massive chest. Burning liquid spread over its body and its flesh exploded with green flames. The beast let out a high-pitched squeal as its leathery flesh melted from its body.

Maor shielded her face from the radiating heat and watched the flames consume the helpless monster before her. After a few moments, Goliath's body fell limp and its cries stopped. The crackling sound of the sizzling flesh ceased as the flames died out and the twitching of its legs stilled. Finally, the bright yellow glow of its eyes extinguished, and silence ensued.

Maor fell to her knees and reached for her police radio as relief overwhelmed her.

"1153 to dispatch," she said, sniffing back the tears.

"Dispatch to 1153, go 'head," the dispatcher responded.

"Ma'am, do you have a report of a fire in the lower Ninth Ward?"

"10-4. Fire, EMS, and police are on their way."

"Ma'am, send me everyone to the levy wall near that same block. I got that son of a bitch. Goliath is dead. I'm on the other side of the wall. North Robertson Street side," Maor informed.

"10-4, ma'am," the dispatcher replied with elation. "All Fifth Precinct units are on the way. I'll notify Car 1 and Car 2 as well."

Maor stood and gasped for breath as she listened to the comforting sound of sirens in the distance. The smell of burning flesh and putrid water had never appealed to her so much, but more importantly, peace filled the darkness once again.

"I'm sorry, James."

CHAPTER THIRTY-EIGHT

"Detective, are you ready?"
—Chief Martel

The thought of wearing a tie irritated Detective Maor. She preferred a cocktail dress and heels on dressy occasions, but that attire could never be allowed or practical as part of the New Orleans Police Department uniform, so the tie would have to do.

Attending any city or department function where full Class B uniform was required did not happen often for Detective Maor. Bar the traditional remembrance ceremonies every so often, female officers were not obligated to wear both the tie and hat, but she had a special day ahead of her after everything that had happened.

"Detective, are you ready?" Chief Martel asked.

"Yes, sir, I'm ready," Maor replied.

Chief Martel stood next to Detective Maor as the mayor spoke over the microphone.

"Without further ado, I present to you the detective who took down two of the city's most vicious murderers, both natural and supernatural, one only hours after being released from the hospital. We owe her. The *city* owes her," the mayor announced, and the crowd of city officials and other officers applauded. "With that said, it is my honor to award Nola Maor with the title of Detective Sergeant and the key to the city!"

Maor walked onto the small stage that had been set up outside the police headquarters and looked out to the city officials and citizens who had attended. Her stomach twinged with nervousness, but she took the trophy key and shook the mayor's hand.

"Thank you," Maor said. "After one of the deadliest summers in the history of New Orleans, the city finds itself mourning its lost citizens and trying to heal from devastation caused by two monsters. The existence of Goliath has opened up a new world to us all. We have to adapt, but the city is strong. Our citizens are strong. We'll grow from this and we will all be more prepared, so this will never happen again. Thank you."

After the worst thirty seconds of her life, Maor rushed off the stage and back to her car, amused at everyone applauding her for simply doing her job.

As Maor drove through the streets of New Orleans, she noticed that the sights and sounds of the city were back to normal. Groups of citizens threw barbecues and block parties, and the city ramped up for carnival season.

While Maor waited at a set of traffic lights and observed the surviving citizens enjoy their neighborhood atmosphere, she pulled a thin gold chain from under her shirt and kissed the golden cross on the end.

"Thank you, Lord," Maor said.

Unashamed to express her newfound beliefs, she rested the cross above her shirt as her police radio beeped.

"In the First District, Signal 34S code 2, male shot at the corner of North Claiborne and Orleans Ave," the dispatcher announced.

"1153," Maor replied.

"Go 'head, 1153," the dispatcher responded.

"Ma'am, I'm free and in the area. Go ahead and send me that way. I'll advise when I arrive."

"10-4, ma'am. I'm sending multiple units that way as well. I know you can handle yourself, but please wait for backup, ma'am. The city needs you," the dispatcher replied.

Maor placed the flashing blue light on her dashboard and initiated her sirens. She took off in the direction of the shooting with a proud smile on her face.

"One thing about you, New Orleans, you're never boring. Let your light shine, even in darkness."

END

NOLA MAOR WILL RETURN.

ABOUT
THE AUTHOR

Ashon Ruffins is a native New Orleanian and a military Veteran. He earned a Master's Degree in Business Administration, while also holding certifications for several other professions. He loves the art of storytelling in all genres and believes the best lessons in life can be told through fiction.

Descent of a Broken Man is his debut novel. Ashon is married and the father of two beautiful children. He also has a passion for the culinary arts. He has to go now—his kids are waiting for him to cook.

Printed in Great Britain
by Amazon

77854657R00129